PULP Literature

PULP LITERATURE PRESS

Issue No. 30, Spring 2021

Publisher: Pulp Literature Press; Managing Editor: Jennifer Landels; Senior Editor: Mel Anastasiou; Acquisitions Editor: Genevieve Wynand; Editor: Jessica Fabrizius; Poetry Editors: Daniel Cowper, Emily Osborne; Assistant Editors: Samantha Olson, Brooklynn Hook, Veronika Kos, Melisa Gruger; Copy Editors: Amanda Bidnall, Mary Rykov; Proofreader: Mary Rykov; Graphic Design: Amanda Bidnall; Cover Design: Kate Landels; First Readers: Carol McCauley, Brenda Carre; Subscriptions: Carol McCauley; Advertising: Samantha Olson. For advertising rates, direct inquiries to info@pulpliterature.com.

Cover painting, *Superbloom* by Weiwei Xu. Artwork for 'O World' by Phoebe Mol. All other illustrations by Mel Anastasiou.

Pulp Literature: ISSN 2292-2164 (Print), ISSN 2292-2172 (Digital), Issue No. 30, Spring 2021.

Published quarterly by Pulp Literature Press, 21955 16 Ave, Langley, BC, Canada V2Z 1K5, pulpliterature.com, at $15.00 per copy. Annual subscription $50.00 in Canada, $68.00 in continental USA, $86.00 elsewhere. Printed in Victoria, BC, Canada, by First Choice Books / Victoria Bindery. Copyright © 2021 Pulp Literature Press. All stories and works of art copyright © 2021 their authors as per bylines.

Pulp Literature Press gratefully acknowledges the support of the Canada Council for the Arts.

Pulp Literature is a proud member of the Magazine Association of BC and Magazines Canada.

TABLE OF CONTENTS

FROM THE PULP LIT PULPIT

The Great Do-Over

Springtime lessons abound: it is the season of rebirth, renewal, hope. It is a growing season. And in my writer's mind, it is the revising season. A reminder that all of life is a rough draft and we often figure things out by saying or doing them badly the first time. But with the flick of a calendar page — or an eraser — transformation is in the offing.

Spring offers a change of scene and scenery. It reminds us that each of us is the author of our own life, and that how we describe and understand that life is an ongoing narrative. We can rewrite the plot and setting as we go. Because brave *re-vision* is both the act of revising and of seeing again — of being again.

Metamorphosis, a thread that runs through many of the stories in this issue, teaches us that we might make mistakes; the process is messy. To become a butterfly, that perennial symbol of metamorphosis, the caterpillar must digest itself, must literally melt, before it grows wings and takes flight.

Of this season of second drafts, Margaret Atwood reminds us: *In the spring, at the end of the day, you should smell like dirt.* Yes. Dig in the dirt. Trudge through the mud. Make a pencil-smudged, crossed-out mess of the page. Do. Do again. Melt. Fly.

~Genevieve Wynand

*I*N THIS ISSUE

Join us as we step into the blossoming spring with *Superbloom*, by cover artist **Weiwei Xu**, and disappear into future past with feature author **Robert Silverberg**'s 'Chip Runner' and **Leo X Robertson**'s 'Bar Hopping for Astronauts'.

Take a deep breath and let the aroma of the blossoms permeate your senses because taste and scents infuse **Michelle Goddard**'s 'Bhut', 'The Shepherdess: Merveilles' by **JM Landels**, and 'The Smell of Screaming' by SiWC runner-up **Adrienne Gruber**.

We witness the powerful and varied effects of death and mourning in 'Life Supports' by **Claire Lawrence**, and in Raven Contest winner 'Good Intentions' by **Nancy Ludmerer**.

We cross the fourth wall in **Erin MacNair**'s Raven Contest runner-up 'It Can Be Done with Words', we cross the desert in **Paige Elizabeth Wajda**'s rhapsodic 'Heaven or Las Vegas', and we cross dimensions in **PG Streeter**'s homage to Shakespeare in 'The Earth Has Bubbles'.

Phoebe Mol washes away her troubles in the graphic version of Edna St Vincent Millay's 'O World', while Marietta puts out fire with gasoline in the next chapter of **Mel Anastasiou**'s *The Extra: Frankie Ray and the Blazing Anubis*.

Pulp Literature Press

Out of the fires of a Caribbean slave revolt, shipwrecked on the jungle coast of 16th-century Ecuador, an educated slave, a shaman, and a monk hunted by the Inquisition fight for freedom against the might of Imperial Spain.

Dive into an epic slipstream novel of intrigue and adventure from fantasy author Matthew Hughes, the writer George R.R. Martin calls 'criminally underrated,' and Robert J. Sawyer says is 'a towering talent.'

'A triumph!' - Cecelia Holland
'Sensational' - Candas Jane Dorsey

pulpliterature.com
Fantastic Fresh Fiction!

CHIP RUNNER

Robert Silverberg

Robert Silverberg is one of the world's most prolific and beloved SF authors. He is a member of the Science Fiction and Fantasy Hall of Fame and an SWFA Grand Master. He has won multiple Hugo and Nebula awards, and has attended every Hugo award ceremony since 1953. Aside from the Majipoor Chronicles, he has published dozens of acclaimed short stories. In 2019 we gave 'The Pope of the Chimps' an afterlife in Pulp Literature Issue 22, and we are delighted to do the same with 'Chip Runner', which was first published in The Microverse, Byron Press, 1989. What was spec fic over thirty years ago has become historical SF in 2021. We hope you enjoy the trip.

Chip Runner

He was fifteen and looked about ninety, and a frail ninety at that. I knew his mother and his father, separately — they were Silicon Valley people, divorced, very important in their respective companies — and separately they had asked me to try to work with him. His skin was blue-grey and tight, drawn cruelly close over the jutting bones of his face. His eyes were grey too, and huge, and they lay deep within their sockets. His arms were like sticks. His thin lips were set in an angry grimace.

The chart before me on my desk told me that he was five feet eight inches tall and weighed 71 pounds. He was in his third year at one of the best private schools in the Palo Alto district. His IQ was 161. He crackled with intelligence and intensity. That was a novelty for me right at the outset. Most of my patients are depressed, withdrawn, uncertain of themselves, elusive, shy: virtual zombies. He wasn't anything like that. There would be other surprises ahead.

"So you're planning to go into the hardware end of the computer industry, your parents tell me," I began. The usual let's-build-a-relationship procedure.

He blew it away instantly with a single sour glare. "Is that your standard opening? 'Tell me all about your favourite hobby, my boy'? If you don't mind, I'd rather skip all the bullshit, doctor, and then we can both get out of here faster. You're supposed to ask me about my eating habits."

It amazed me to see him trying to take control of the session this way within the first thirty seconds. I marvelled at how different he was from most of the others, the poor sad wispy creatures who force me to fish for every word.

"Actually, I do enjoy talking about the latest developments in the world of computers, too," I said, still working hard at being genial.

"But my guess is you don't talk about them very often, or you wouldn't call it 'the hardware end'. Or 'the computer industry'. We don't use mundo phrases like those anymore." His high thin voice sizzled with barely suppressed rage. "Come on, doctor. Let's get right down to it. You think I'm anorexic, don't you?"

"Well—"

"I know about anorexia. It's a mental disease of girls, a vanity thing. They starve themselves because they want to look beautiful, and they can't bring themselves to realize that they're not too fat. Vanity isn't the issue for me. And I'm not a girl, doctor. Even you ought to be able to see that right away."

"Timothy—"

"I want to let you know right out front that I don't have an eating disorder and I don't belong in a shrink's office. I know exactly what I'm doing all the time. The only reason I came today is to get my mother off my back, because she's taken it into her head that I'm trying to starve myself to death. She said I had to come here and see you. So I'm here. All right?"

"All right," I said, and stood up. I am a tall man, deep-chested, very broad through the shoulders. I can loom when necessary. A flicker of fear crossed Timothy's face, which was the effect I wanted to produce. When it's appropriate for the therapist to assert authority, simple-minded methods are often the most effective. "Let's talk about eating, Timothy. What did you have for lunch today?"

He shrugged. "A piece of bread. Some lettuce."

"That's all?"

"A glass of water."

"And for breakfast?"

"I don't eat breakfast."

"But you'll have a substantial dinner, won't you?"

"Maybe some fish. Maybe not. I think food is pretty gross."

I nodded. "Could you operate your computer with the power turned off, Timothy?"

"Isn't that a pretty condescending sort of question, doctor?"

"I suppose it is. Okay, I'll be more direct. Do you think you can run your body without giving it any fuel?"

"My body runs just fine," he said, with a defiant edge.

"Does it? What sports do you play?"

"Sports?" It might have been a Martian word.

"You know, the normal weight for someone of your age and height ought to be——"

"There's nothing normal about me, doctor. Why should my weight be any more normal than the rest of me?"

"It was until last year, apparently. Then you stopped eating. Your family is worried about you, you know."

"I'll be okay," he said sullenly.

"You want to stay healthy, don't you?"

He stared at me for a long chilly moment. There was something close to hatred in his eyes, or so I imagined.

"What I want is to disappear," he said.

That night, I dreamed I was disappearing. I stood naked and alone on a slab of grey metal in the middle of a vast empty plain under a sinister coppery sky, and I began steadily to shrink. I grew smaller and smaller. Pores appeared on the surface of the metal slab and widened into jagged craters, and then into great crevices and gullies. A cloud of luminous dust shimmered about my head. Grains of sand, specks, mere motes, now took on the aspect of immense boulders. Down I drifted, gliding into the darkness of a fathomless chasm. Creatures I had not noticed before hovered about me, astonishing monsters, hairy, many-legged. They made menacing gestures, but I slipped away, downward, downward, and they were gone. The air was alive now with vibrating particles, inanimate, furious, that danced in frantic zigzag patterns, veering wildly past me, now and again crashing into me, knocking my breath from me, sending me ricocheting for what seemed like miles. I was floating, spinning, tumbling with no control. Pulsating waves of blinding light pounded me. I was falling into the infinitely small, and there was no halting my descent. I would shrink and shrink and shrink until I slipped through the realm of matter entirely and was lost. A mob of contemptuous glowing things — electrons and protons, maybe, but how could I tell? — crowded close around me, emitting fizzy sparks that seemed to me like jeers and laughter. They told me to keep moving along, to get myself out of their kingdom, or I would meet a terrible death. "To see a world in a grain of sand," Blake wrote. Yes. And Eliot wrote, "I will show you fear in a handful of dust." I went on downward, and downward still. And then I awoke gasping, drenched in sweat, terrified, alone.

Normally the patient is uncommunicative. You interview parents, siblings, teachers, friends, anyone who might provide a clue or an opening wedge. The patients have lost all sense of a normal body image and ignore the food-deprivation prompts that a normal body gives its owner. Food is the enemy. Food must be resisted. They eat only when forced to, and then as little as possible. They are unaware that they are frighteningly gaunt. Strip them and put them in front of a mirror, and they will pinch their sagging empty skin to show you imaginary fatty bulges. Sometimes the process of self-skeletonization is impossible to halt, even by therapy. When it reaches a certain point, the degree of organic damage becomes irreversible and the death spiral begins.

"He was always tremendously bright," Timothy's mother said. She was fifty, a striking woman, trim, elegant, almost radiant, vice-president of finance at one of the biggest Valley companies. I knew her in that familiarly involuted California way: her present husband used to be married to my first wife. "A genius, his teachers all said. But strange, you know? Moody. Dreamy. I used to think he was on drugs, though of course none of the kids do that anymore." Timothy was her only child by her first marriage. "It scares me to death to watch him wasting away like that. When I see him, I want to take him and shake him and force ice cream down his throat. Pasta, milkshakes, anything. And then I want to hold him, and I want to cry."

"You'd think he'd be starting to shave by now," his father said. Technical man, working on nanoengineering projects at the Stanford AI lab. We often played racquetball together. "I was. You too, probably. I got a look at him in the shower, three or four months ago. Hasn't even reached puberty yet. Fifteen and not a hair on him. It's the starvation, isn't it? It's retarding his physical development, right?"

"I keep trying to get him to, like, eat something, anything," his stepbrother Mick said. "He lives with us, you know, on the weekends, and most of the time he's downstairs playing with his computers, but sometimes I can get him to go out with us, and we buy, like, a chilli dog for him or, you know, a burrito, and he goes, Thank you, thank you, and pretends to eat it, but then he throws it away when he thinks we're not looking. He is *so* weird, you know? And scary. You look at him with those ribs and all, and he's like something out of a horror movie."

"What I want is to disappear," Timothy said.

He came every Tuesday and Thursday for one-hour sessions. There was at the beginning an undertone of hostility and suspicion to everything he said. I asked him, in my layman way, a few things about the latest developments in computers, and he answered me in monosyllables at first, not at all bothering to hide his disdain for my ignorance and my innocence. But now and again some question of mine would catch his interest, and he would forget to be irritated and would reply at length, going on and on into realms I could not even pretend to understand. Trying to find things of that sort to ask him seemed my best avenue of approach. But of course I knew I was unlikely to achieve anything of therapeutic value if we simply talked about computers for the whole hour.

He was very guarded, as was only to be expected, when I would bring the conversation around to the topic of eating. He made it clear that his eating habits were his own business and he would rather not discuss them with me, or anyone. Yet there was an aggressive glow on his face whenever we spoke of the way he ate that called Kafka's hunger artist to my mind: he seemed proud of his achievements in starvation, even eager to be admired for his skill at shunning food.

Too much directness in the early stages of therapy is generally counterproductive where anorexia is the problem. Patients *love* their syndrome and resist any therapeutic approach that might deprive them of it. Timothy and I talked mainly of his studies, his classmates, his stepbrothers. Progress was slow, circuitous, agonizing. What was most agonizing was my realization that I didn't have much time. According to the report from his school physician, he was already running at dangerously low levels, bones weakening, muscles degenerating, electrolyte balance cock-eyed, hormonal systems in disarray. The necessary treatment before long would be hospitalization, not psychotherapy, and it might almost be too late even for that.

He was aware that he was wasting away and in danger. He didn't seem to care.

It was the fifth session now, and I sensed that his armour might be ready to crack. As a psychologist whose role it is to help people, I had some scientific interest in finding out what made him tick — not particularly for his sake, but for the sake of other patients who might be more interested in being helped. He could relate to that. His facial expressions changed. He became less hostile. He was starting to think of me not as a member of the enemy but as a neutral observer, a dispassionate investigator. The next step was to make him see me as an ally. You and me, Timothy, standing together against *them*. I told him a few things about myself, my childhood, my troubled adolescence: little nuggets of confidence, offered by way of trade. I let him see that I wasn't going to force anything on him. So far as I was concerned, I told him, he was basically free to starve himself to death if that was what he was really after.

"When you disappear," I said finally, "where is it that you want to go?"

The moment was ripe, and the breakthrough went beyond my highest expectations.

"You know what a microchip is?" he asked.

"Sure."

"I go down into them."

Not I *want* to go down into them. But I *do* go down into them.

"Tell me about that," I said.

"The only way you can understand the nature of reality," he said, "is to take a close look at it. To really and truly take a look, you know? Here we have these fantastic chips, a whole processing unit smaller than your little toenail with fifty times the data-handling capacity of the old mainframes. What goes on inside them? I mean, what *really* goes on? I go into them and I look. It's like a trance, you know? You sharpen your concentration, and you sharpen it and sharpen it, and then you're moving downward, inward, deeper and deeper."

He laughed harshly. "You think this is all mystical ka-ka, don't you? Half of you thinks I'm just a crazy kid mouthing off, and the other half thinks, here's a kid who's smart as hell, feeding you a line of malarkey to keep you away from the real topic. Right, doctor? Right?"

"I had a dream a couple of weeks ago about shrinking down into the infinitely small," I said. "A nightmare, really. But a fascinating one. Fascinating and frightening both. I went all the way down to the molecular level, past grains of sand, past bacteria, down to electrons and protons, or what I suppose were electrons and protons."

"What was the light like, where you were?"

"Blinding. It came in pulsing waves."

"What colour?"

"Every colour all at once," I said.

He stared at me. "No shit!"

"Is that the way it looks for you?"

"Yes. No." He shifted uneasily. "How can I tell if you saw what I saw? But it's a stream of colours, yes. Pulsing. And—all the colours at once, yes, that's how you could describe it—"

"Tell me more."

"More what?"

"When you go downward—tell me what it's like, Timothy."

He gave me his lofty look, his pedagogic look. "You know how small a chip is? A MOSFET, say?"

"MOSFET?"

"Metal-oxide-silicon field-effect transistor," he said. "The newest ones have a minimum feature size of about a micrometre. Ten to the minus sixth metres. That's a millionth of a metre, all right? Small. It isn't down there on the molecular level, no. You could fit 200 amœbas into a MOSFET channel one micrometre long. Okay? Okay? Or a whole army of viruses. But it's still plenty small. That's where I go. And I run down the corridors of the chips, with electrons whizzing by me all the time. Of course, I can't see them. Even a lot smaller, you can't see electrons; you can only compute the probabilities of their paths. But you can feel them. *I* can feel them. And I run among them, everywhere, through the corridors, through the channels, past the gates, past the open spaces in the lattice. Getting to know the territory. Feeling at home in it."

"What's an electron like, when you feel it?"

"You dreamed it, you said. You tell me."

"Sparks," I said. "Something fizzy, going by in a blur."

"You read about that somewhere, in one of your journals?"

"It's what I saw," I said. "What I felt, when I had that dream."

"But that's it! That's it exactly!" He was perspiring. His face was flushed. His hands were trembling. His whole body was ablaze with a metabolic fervour I had not previously seen in him. He looked like a skeleton who had just trotted off a basketball court after a hard game. He leaned toward me and said, looking suddenly vulnerable in a way that he had never allowed himself to seem with me before, "Are you sure it was only a dream? Or do you go there too?"

He began to look healthier. There was some colour in his cheeks now, and he seemed more relaxed, less twitchy. I had the feeling that he was putting on a little weight, although the medical reports I was getting from his school physician didn't confirm that in any significant way — some weeks he'd be up a pound or two, some weeks down, and there was never any net gain. His mother reported that he went through periods when he appeared to be showing a little interest in food, but these were usually followed by periods of rigorous fasting or at best his typical sort of reluctant nibbling. There was nothing in any of this that I could find tremendously encouraging, but I had the definite feeling that I was starting to reach him, that I was beginning to win him back from the brink.

Timothy said, "I have to be weightless in order to get there. I mean, literally weightless. Where I am now, it's only a beginning. I need to lose all the rest."

"Only a beginning," I said, appalled, and jotted a few quick notes.

"I've attained take-off capability. But I can never get far enough. I run into a barrier on the way down, just as I'm entering the truly structural regions of the chip."

"Yet you do get right into the interior of the chip."

"Into it, yes. But I don't attain the real understanding that I'm after. Perhaps the problem's in the chip itself, not in me. Maybe if I tried a quantum-well chip instead of a MOSFET I'd get where I want to go, but they aren't ready yet, or if they are I don't have any way of getting my hands on one. I want to ride the probability waves, do you see? I want to be small enough to grab hold of an electron and stay with it as it zooms through the lattice."

His eyes were blazing. "Try talking about this stuff with my brother. Or anyone. The ones who don't understand think I'm crazy. So do the ones who do."

"You can talk here, Timothy."

"The chip, the integrated circuit—what we're really talking about is transistors, microscopic ones, maybe a billion of them arranged side by side. Silicon or germanium, doped with impurities like boron, arsenic, sometimes other things. On one side are the N-type charge carriers, and the P-type ones are on the other, with an insulating layer between; and when the voltage comes through the gate, the electrons migrate to the P-type side, because it's positively charged, and the holes, the zones of positive charge, go to the N-type side. So your basic logic circuit—" He paused. "You following this?"

"More or less. Tell me about what you feel as you start to go downward into a chip."

It begins, he told me, with a rush, an upward surge of almost ecstatic force: he is not descending but floating. The floor falls away beneath him as he dwindles. Then comes the intensifying of perception, dust motes quivering and twinkling in what had a moment before seemed nothing but empty air, and the light taking on strange new refractions and shimmerings. The solid world begins to alter. Familiar shapes — the table, a chair, the computer before him — vanish as he comes closer to their essence. What he sees now is detailed structure, the intricacy of surfaces: no longer a forest, only trees. Everything is texture and there is no solidity. Wood and metal become strands and webs and mazes. Canyons yawn. Abysses open. He goes inward, drifting, tossed like a feather on the molecular breeze.

It is no simple journey. The world grows grainy. He fights his way through a dust storm of swirling granules of oxygen and nitrogen, an invisible blizzard battering him at every step. Ahead lies the chip he seeks, a magnificent thing, a gleaming radiant Valhalla. He begins to run toward it, heedless of obstacles. Giant rainbows sweep the sky: dizzying floods of pure colour, hammering down with a force capable of deflecting the wandering atoms. And then — then —

The chip stands before him like some temple of Zeus rising on the Athenian plain. Giant glowing columns, yawning gateways, dark beckoning corridors, hidden sanctuaries — beyond access, beyond comprehension. It glimmers with light of many colours. A strange swelling music fills the air. He feels like an explorer taking the first stumbling steps into a lost world. And he is still shrinking.

The intricacies of the chip swell, surging like metal fungi filling with water after a rain: they spring higher and higher, darkening the sky, concealing it entirely. Another level downward and he is barely large enough to manage the passage across the threshold, but he does, and enters. Here he can move freely.

He is in a strange canyon whose silvery walls, riven with vast fissures, rise farther than he can see. He runs. He runs. He has infinite energy; his legs move like springs. Behind him the gates open, close, open, close. Rivers of torrential current surge through, lifting him, carrying him along. He senses, does not see, the vibrating of the atoms of silicon or boron; he senses, does not see, the electrons and the not-electrons flooding past, streaming toward the sides, positive or negative, to which they are inexorably drawn.

But there is more. He runs on and on and on. There is infinitely more, a world within this world, a world that lies at his feet and mocks him with its inaccessibility. It swirls before him, a whirl-pool, a maelstrom. He would throw himself into it if he could, but some invisible barrier keeps him from it. This is as far as he can go. This is as much as he can achieve. He yearns to reach out, pluck an electron from its path as it goes careening past, and stare into its heart. He wants to step inside the atoms and breathe the mysterious air within their boundaries. He longs to look upon their hidden nuclei. He hungers for the sight of mesons, quarks, neutrinos. There is more, always more, an unending series of worlds within worlds, and he is huge, he is impossibly clumsy, he is a lurching reeling mountainous titan, incapable of penetrating beyond this point—

So far, and no farther—

No farther—

He looked up at me from the far side of the desk. Sweat was streaming down his face, and his light shirt was clinging to his skin. That sallow cadaverous look was gone from him entirely. He looked transfigured, aflame, throbbing with life: more alive than anyone I had ever seen, or so it seemed to me in that moment. There was a Faustian fire in his look, a world-swallowing urgency. Magellan must have looked that way sometimes, or Newton, or Galileo. And then in a moment more it was gone, and all I saw before me was a miserable scrawny boy, shrunken, feeble, pitifully frail.

I went to talk to a physicist I knew, a friend of Timothy's father who did advanced research at the university. I said nothing about Timothy to him.

"What's a quantum well?" I asked him.

He looked puzzled. "Where'd you hear of those?"

"Someone I know. But I couldn't follow much of what he was saying."

"Extremely small switching device," he said. "Experimental, maybe five, ten years away. Less if we're very lucky. The idea is that you use two different semiconductive materials in a single crystal lattice, a superlattice, something like a three-dimensional checkerboard. Electrons tunnelling between squares could be made to perform digital operations at tremendous speeds."

"And how small would this thing be, compared with the sort of transistors they have on chips now?"

"It would be down in the nanometre range," he told me. "That's a billionth of a metre. Smaller than a virus. Getting right down there close to the theoretical limits for semiconductivity. Any smaller and you'll be measuring things in angstroms."

"Angstroms?"

"One ten-billionth of a metre. We measure the diameter of atoms in angstrom units."

"Ah," I said. "All right. Can I ask you something else?"

He looked amused, patient, tolerant.

"Does anyone know much about what an electron looks like?"

"*Looks* like?"

"Its physical appearance. I mean, has any sort of work been done on examining them, maybe even photographing them——"

"You know about the uncertainty principle?" he asked.

"Well——not much, really——"

"Electrons are very damned tiny. They've got a mass of—— ah——about nine times ten to the minus twenty-eighth grams. We need light in order to see, in any sense of the word. We see by receiving light radiated by an object, or by hitting it with light and getting a reflection. The smallest unit of light we can use, which is the photon, has such a long wavelength that it would completely hide an electron from view, so to speak. And we can't use radiation of shorter wavelength——gammas, let's say, or X-rays——for making our measurements, either, because the shorter the wavelength the greater the energy, and so a gamma ray would simply kick any electron we were going to inspect to hell and gone. So we can't *see* electrons. The very act of determining their position imparts new velocity to them, which alters their position. The best we can do by way of examining electrons is make an enlightened guess, a probabilistic determination, of where they are and how fast they're moving. In a very rough way, that's what we mean by the uncertainty principle."

"You mean in order to look an electron in the eye, you'd have to be the size of an electron yourself? Or even smaller?"

He gave me a strange look. "I suppose that question makes sense," he said. "And I suppose I could answer yes to it. But what the hell are we talking about, now?"

I dreamed again that night: a feverish, disjointed dream of gigantic grotesque creatures shining with a fluorescent glow against a sky blacker than any night. They had claws, tentacles, eyes by the dozens. Their swollen asymmetrical bodies were bristling with thick red hairs. Some were clad in thick armour, others were equipped with ugly shining spikes that jutted in rows of ten or twenty from their quivering skins. They were pursuing me through the airless void. Wherever I ran there were more of them, crowding close. Behind them I saw the walls of the cosmos beginning to shiver and flow. The sky itself was dancing. Colour was breaking through the blackness: eddying bands of every hue at once, interwoven like great chains. I ran, and I ran, and I ran, but there were monsters on every side, and no escape.

Timothy missed an appointment. For some days now he had been growing more distant, often simply sitting silently, staring at me for the whole hour out of some hermetic sphere of unapproachability. That struck me as nothing more than predictable passive-aggressive resistance, but when he failed to show up at all I was startled: such blatant rebellion wasn't his expectable mode. Some alternative therapeutic strategies seemed in order: more direct intervention with me playing the role of a gruff, loving older brother, or perhaps family therapy. Despite his recent aloofness, I still felt I could get to him in time. But this business of skipping appointments was unacceptable. I phoned his mother the next day, only to learn that he was in the hospital. After my last patient of the morning, I drove across town to see him. The attending physician, a chunky-faced resident, turned frosty when I told him that I was Timothy's therapist, that I had been treating him for anorexia. I didn't need to be telepathic to know that he was thinking, *You didn't do much of a job with him, did you?*

"His parents are with him now," he told me. "Let me find out if they want you to go in."

Actually, they were all there: parents, stepparents, the various children by the various second marriages. Timothy seemed to be no more than a waxen doll. They had brought him books, tapes, even a laptop computer, but everything was pushed to the corners of the bed. The shrunken figure in the middle barely raised the level of the coverlet a few inches. They had him on an IV unit, and a webwork of lines and cables ran to him from the array of medical machines surrounding him. Timothy's eyes were open, but he seemed to be staring into some other world, perhaps that same world of rampaging bacteria and quivering molecules that had haunted my sleep a few nights before. He seemed to be smiling.

"He collapsed at school," his mother whispered.

"In the computer lab, no less," said his father, with a nervous ratcheting laugh. "He was last conscious about two hours ago, but he wasn't talking coherently."

"He wants to go inside his computer," one of the little boys said. "That's crazy, isn't it?" He might have been seven.

"Timothy's going to die, Timothy's going to die," chanted somebody's daughter.

"Christopher! Bree! Shhh, both of you!" said three of the various parents, all at once.

"Has he started to respond to the IV?" I asked.

"They don't think so. It's not at all good," his mother said. "He's right on the edge. He lost three pounds this week. We thought he was eating, but he must have been sliding the food into his pocket, or something like that." She shook her head. "You can't be a policeman."

Her eyes were cold. So were her husband's, and even those of the stepparents. Telling me, *This is your fault, we counted on you to make him stop starving himself.* What could I say? You can only heal the ones you can reach. Timothy had been determined to keep himself beyond my grasp. Still, I felt the keenness of their reproachful anger, and it hurt.

"I've seen worse cases than this reverse under medical treatment," I told them. "They'll build up his strength until he's capable of talking with me again. And then I'm certain I'll be able to lick this thing. I was just beginning to break through his defences when—when he—"

Sure. It costs no more to give them a little optimism. I gave them what I could: experience with other cases of severe food deprivation, positive results following a severe crisis of this nature, et cetera, et cetera, the man of science dipping into his reservoir of experience. They all began to brighten as I spoke. They even managed to convince themselves that a little colour was coming into Timothy's cheeks, that he was stirring, that he might soon be regaining consciousness as the machinery surrounding him pumped the nutrients he had so conscientiously forbidden himself to have.

"Look," this one said, or that one. "Look how he's moving his hands! Look how he's breathing. It's better, isn't it?"

I actually began to believe it myself.

But then I heard his dry thin voice echoing in the caverns of my mind: *I can never get far enough. I have to be weightless in order to get there. Where I am now, it's only a beginning. I need to lose all the rest.*

I want to disappear.

That night, a third dream, vivid, precise, concrete. I was falling and running at the same time, my legs pistoning like those of a marathon runner in the twenty-sixth mile while simultaneously I dropped in free fall through airless dark toward the silver-black surface of some distant world. And fell and fell and fell, in utter weightlessness, and hit the surface easily and kept on running, moving not forward but downward, the atoms of the ground parting for me as I ran. I became smaller as I descended, and smaller yet, and even smaller, until I was a mere phantom, a running ghost, the bodiless idea of myself. And still I went downward toward the dazzling heart of things, shorn now of all impediments of the flesh.

I phoned the hospital the next morning. Timothy had died a little after dawn.

Did I fail with him? Well, then, I failed. But I think no one could possibly have succeeded. He went where he wanted to go; and so great was the force of his will that any attempts at impeding him must have seemed to him like the mere buzzings of insects: meaningless, insignificant.

So now his purpose is achieved. He has shed his useless husk. He has gone on, floating, running, descending: downward, inward, toward the core, where knowledge is absolute and uncertainty is unknown. He is running among the shining electrons now. He is down there among the angstrom units at last.

FEATURE INTERVIEW

Robert Silverberg

Pulp Literature: In 'Chip Runner' you weave together mental illness and technology. Could you tell us a bit about the inspiration for this story?

Robert Silverberg: Everybody was getting PCs around then and talking computer stuff all the time. And the woman I was keeping company with in that era was a therapist specializing in eating disorders. So if I didn't hear about one thing, it was the other. Natural combination.

PL: Published in 1989 on the cusp of Web 1.0, and reprinted here at the dawn of Web 5.0, 'Chip Runner' does feel like technological fulfillment—so much of who we are in 2021 is stored in bytes, with all of us now drops in the cloud. What do you think of this emerging entanglement of identity and technology?

RS: We are really entangled, aren't we? But there's no turning back. And though I dislike a lot of the stuff the omnipresent social media force upon us, it's wonderful to get a reprint query from China in the morning, say yes by lunchtime, and have the contract before dinner.

PL: The narrator in 'Chip Runner' maintains a curious but necessarily clinical fascination with his patient, and does identify, through his own dreams, with some of Timothy's experience. Are there any parallels here with the relationship between writer and reader? What does a writer owe their readers?

RS: I don't think the writer owes the reader anything but professional competence in storytelling, which I have tried to deliver for the past sixty-plus years.

PL: *Could you tell us a bit about your journey from sci-fi fan to Grand Master?*

RS: I thought I could be a pretty good science fiction writer one day, and after a while I was. It has been an interesting trip.

PL: *With a decades-long writing career, you've surely witnessed waxing and waning in many corners of the SF market. Does anything in particular stand out to you?*

RS: Been a lot of waxing and waning, all right, but I prefer not to open this particular can of worms, metaphors be damned, right now.

PL: *Ursula K Le Guin has said that "science fiction is not prescriptive; it is descriptive." Do you agree with her? When did you first learn that writing in the genre holds unique power?*

RS: It's nearly always descriptive — we can only write about the world we live in. There are some remarkable exceptions, such as Murray Leinster's astonishing 1946 story, 'A Logic Named Joe', which predicts the whole Internet right down to Google, and vividly shows how dependent we will be on it. But most SF is firmly rooted in its own era, whatever the writer may think, and so be it.

PL*: In a recent interview with the* Los Angeles Review of Books, *you said, "We are all products of the Zeitgeist." What might that mean for writers writing — and readers reading — in these pandemic days? What has this meant for you?*

RS: I suppose we will be writing about pandemics for a while. But I've just been looking at a 1973 story of mine, 'This Is the Road', that was reprinted in an anthology designed to produce funds for COVID testing. It depicts a world that has suddenly fallen into a shambles. The details are different but the effect is just as devastating. *Nothing new under the sun*, the poet said, and he was right.

PL*: Thank you for making the time to speak with us. Before we go, could you tell us about your current projects?*

RS: I retired from writing about a decade ago. I'm 86 years old. My current project is survival.

THE EXTRA: FRANKIE RAY AND THE BLAZING ANUBIS

Mel Anastasiou

Mel Anastasiou writes mysteries, including the Fairmount Manor Mysteries and the Hertfordshire Pub Mysteries, available at pulpliterature.com. For her novel Stella Ryman and the Fairmount Manor Mysteries, Mel won a Literary Titan Gold Book Award and was longlisted for the Leacock Memorial Medal for Humour.

The Extra:
A Monument Studios Mystery

In this the latest episode of The Extra: A Monument Studios Mystery, *set in 1934 silver-screen Hollywood, Frankie Ray, disguised as a male detective, will stop at nothing to clear her name in the murder of film star Gilbert Howard. As the police close in on her, Frankie pursues her only remaining witness with the help of her ally, Eugene Ellery. But finding the elusive girl with whom Howard spent his last night is proving more of a struggle than she expected.*

Chapter One

Frankie had trouble getting the Model A started. She fiddled with the mix, got the choke and the ignition backward, and prayed that the engine wouldn't flood. When at last it started, she hit a curb pulling out onto Sunset Boulevard, so that the back wheel slammed up and then down again with a shrill complaint of springs. The rumble seat popped open with a *thunk*. Adrenalin pumping, she rode the clutch the way Connie had taught her in the back alley at home in Vancouver, where chickens shrieked and fluttered out of the Model A's way and not a garbage can in the neighbourhood was spared.

Both hands on the wheel, she steered straight along Sunset Boulevard. Monument Studios, with its formidable angels, appeared and then vanished on her left. She passed the brothel with its glowing yellow windows and safe, friendly air. More of Hollywood's illusions.

She kept a heavy foot on the gas and sped through the shadows. She nearly missed the sign for Paradise Gardens, so that at the last second she skewed between two parked cars at a shockingly bad angle. Frankie decided that neither she nor Frank Achilles gave a cool nickel. She switched off the ignition, walked around the rear of the Model A, and slammed the rumble seat shut.

"All I have to do," she muttered, "is find out whether Eugene tracked down the golden swimmer who loved Gilbert Howard. Then Eugene can tell the police. And I can go home to Vancouver."

She would say thanks and farewell to Eugene and the Queen. Then she would find something she'd always heard of but never been inside—an all-night hockshop. She had something valuable that she might sell for gas money to get home. The diamond in her engagement ring was just a chip. "But the ring itself is gold. Fourteen-carat!" Champ had so informed her the first time he'd slid it onto her finger and asked her never to take it off.

She felt in her right pocket for her engagement ring. When she didn't find it right away, she told herself not to panic, but her heart beat faster as she fumbled her way past the gun into the deepest area of her pocket. It was empty. Hastily, she felt the inside of her left-hand pocket, but found only a pinch of lint.

She growled, "Men have such a lot of pockets. It is entirely ridiculous over-tailoring!"

She fumbled her way through each pocket with no result at all. The ring was gone. The disappointment was too much to bear. And that was when somebody shone a bright light into her eyes.

She held up a hand against the glare. "Watch where you're pointing that thing, buddy."

A male voice invited her to step away from the car.

She reminded herself to keep her temper and her head about her. This was a free country, darn it all, and a citizen had a right to park on any public thoroughfare.

She said, "What's it all about, Officer? Can a man about town help in any way?"

"We've got an investigation rolling, and I'm looking for witnesses. Do you live at Paradise Gardens?"

Frankie coughed. "Nope. What's the case, Officer?"

"Can't say, sir." The policeman added, "We're looking for a young, dark-haired, out-of-town girl. Seen any girls like that?"

"Can't say as I have." Inspired in perhaps equal measures by fury at the intransigent single-bloody-mindedness of the police and a wish to appear urbane and witty, she asked, "Out-of-town girl, is she? Have you searched out of town?"

"Look, you. No nonsense, please," the policeman said. "I've got a report to write up in about ten minutes or the captain will hang my ears from his belt buckle. What's your name and address?"

Frankie's knees inside the grey suiting were none too sure of themselves.

As the man about town, she said, "Well, here's how it is, Officer. I've come to Paradise Gardens to see a friend of the gentler sex. And I'd rather not give my name or my address, as there's a different little woman at my home address who might require a full and lengthy explanation. You understand, Officer."

The policeman sighed as if his pockets were full of second-hand woes. Frankie would like to have informed him that no matter how depressing the policeman's circumstances might be, they were honey compared to being hunted day and night for a crime one hadn't committed.

The policeman asked, "Are you drunk, young fellow?"

Did she dare to attempt the portrayal of a drunken man about town? "Yessir. I'm drunk as Methuselah's doctor."

"Away you go, then, mister, and sleep it off."

Blinking, Frankie looked from the car to the Paradise Gardens sign. "Where do you suggest I go to sleep?"

The policeman said, "If it was me, buddy, I'd go where judgment and imprecation were thinnest on the ground."

Frankie bowed unsteadily. "Thank you, Officer. Carry on with your hallowed task, protecting us from out-of-town girls."

As she walked away, Frankie wished she were wearing a hat—a man's hat, not her squashy one—so that she could raise it a little too high. Her stage training told her that the best way to look drunk was to try not to look drunk, which was complicated in this case by also having to try not to look afraid. She stumbled a little under the swinging sign and passed through, along the path among the bungalows, past Villa 12B where the noisy blonde threw things at people. At the spot where the main pathway through the bungalows branched into the paths for Villas 7A and B, she paused. Here she was, on her own again under the deep, dark California sky. *Alone, alone, all, all alone.* The Ancient Mariner had gotten that right. Above her a bird fluttered — no, a bat. With a weighted flick it slipped past her ear and up over Villa 7A so quickly that she had no time to shiver as its passing lifted the ends of her puffball hair.

The little brick path ran from the toes of her shoes toward the central brickwork patio. It split to lead straight to Eugene Ellery's front door. She shoved her hands into her pockets and polished the toes of her brogues on the back of her trouser legs. All her earlier distrust of Eugene seemed now the nerves of a foolish young girl. Pretending to be a man all day had somehow made her feel more of a grown woman, one who could think for herself.

She took the path to Villa 7A and Eugene Ellery's front door. A part of her, the weary part, wondered whether Eugene Ellery might not take charge of everything and save her bacon for her. She pictured herself in the passenger seat of the Model A, with Eugene at the wheel, motoring up the long sunny highway to Vancouver.

But Eugene's front window was dark. Disappointment nearly overcame her, but she realized that he might still be home, in another room in the little bungalow. She took a couple of steps around the corner and sure enough, his bathroom light was on. She gazed at the window with its glowing curtain, yellow against the dark exterior wall. A symbol, perhaps, of hope — of Eugene finding the witness to clear her name. A golden light, a golden swimmer. All things seemed possible when a window glowed against the darkness.

Then the click from Eugene's front door brought her running back around to the front of the villa.

"Frankie, I'm sorry." Eugene stood in his darkened doorway. "I didn't find that blonde woman you're looking for. The one who was swimming with Gilbert Howard the night he died. The police will find her, sometime soon. I'll make sure that you know when they do. Leave Hollywood. Go home."

A light breeze lifted the leaves of a nearby palm and let them fall again with a gentle pattering that reminded her of Vancouver rain. Inside her pockets, she made two fists. She would not cry.

"Leave Hollywood?" she asked. *Without you?*

"Yes. Be careful, and drive like the wind. The police will never find you in Vancouver, because nobody at Paradise Gardens will ever tell them they saw you." He lifted a hand in farewell, and the door snicked shut.

And at that moment, as if written upon the closed door of Villa 7A, the solution to the problem of the blonde swimmer came to her.

No, it didn't *come to her*. Like Cinderella, it struck her for twelve. Frankie had a sudden, crazy desire to laugh, but she couldn't quite manage it. She and Eugene had been looking for the wrong blonde. Gilbert Howard's true love, the faceless golden swimmer.

Perhaps not so faceless! How had she overlooked the obvious? There was a blonde woman nearby, in Villa 12A in Paradise Gardens. The blonde in 12A — the shouter, the thrower of plates, the passionate one — must be the woman Gilbert Howard came to Paradise Gardens to see. *She* was the one who visited him when she wanted to swim in the turquoise pool next door. Although Frankie had caught only glimpses of the blonde in 12A, she knew she would have no difficulty recognizing the young woman's slim figure and cropped, boyish haircut.

Frankie turned on her heel and strode back along the walk toward Villa 12A. A jazzy piano piece spiralled out a side window. The best way to approach the blonde would be a swift attack. Frankie would accuse her straight out and leave the woman no choice but to stammer out her story, and possibly even her guilt. As for clearing Frankie's name, she would have to force the blonde to come with her to the police to tell them her story. Then down at the station among the boys in blue, Frankie would have two choices: reveal her true identity and trust the coils of justice to release her on the blonde's testimony, or continue in the guise of Frank Achilles while the golden swimmer testified and Frankie's name was cleared. The first option was as dicey as anything she'd ever dared in her life. The second option — remaining disguised — was safer, but as Frank Achilles, she would have no opportunity to argue her own innocence.

If there was a third way, she'd think of it. In the meantime, if she had to use force to get the girl to talk to the police, she still had the gun in her pocket. Frankie knocked at the door of 12A.

A voice from inside called out, "Keep your trousers on." Frankie, increasingly impatient, heard the sound of kitchen pots crashing to the floor and a steady string of words she'd last heard from Billie, and before that from her father, Sheridan D. At last the door opened, and a blonde woman in a green dress leaned against the jamb and asked, "What's cooking, brother?"

Frankie stared. It was not out of the question that those long curls were false and that underneath them lay the short pale locks she'd seen on the girl in the pool. But the green dress this blonde in 12A wore would have fit Connie's mother equally well. Without Frankie ever having had a good look at the golden girl's face that night by the pool, she knew this blowsy blonde could not possibly be the slender young woman who had kissed Gilbert Howard so passionately the night he died.

"I'm sorry," Frankie managed to say. She heard the female tones of her voice, and added in her tenor, "You're not the one."

The blonde said, "Don't be sorry, fella. You're not the one for me, either." She threw back her head and laughed, her bosom bouncing heavily under the green bodice. She slammed the door shut, and Frankie found herself alone again in the night.

On shaky legs, she walked through Paradise Gardens toward Villas 7A and B. Eugene's house was dark again except for his bathroom window. Inside, light bloomed and vanished as the bathroom curtains moved in the breeze. She stopped to watch, thinking one clear thought over and over, like the stroke of the bell that ends the day: *With all my hard work and positive attitude, how can I still be in such a fix?*

The breeze picked up slightly, and Frankie took a deep breath of the gardenia-scented air. The perfumes from the white-flowered shrubs smelled stronger at night, she decided, and then the breeze lifted the curtain of Eugene Ellery's bathroom and showed her a brief view of its occupant.

Frankie took a step back, stricken to her centre by the image of the young woman, slender and golden, in Eugene's bathroom. The young, blonde woman stood with her back to the window, drying herself with a towel.

This was the girl she was after—the golden girl who'd kissed Gilbert Howard and then dived into the water while he declaimed murder down upon himself. The girl she'd been looking for was standing naked in Eugene Ellery's bungalow bathroom. And not only that—she must have been in the bathroom a few minutes before, when Eugene answered the door in his shirtsleeves. The blonde must have been inside the house when Eugene had told Frankie that he had not found her.

Another bat flew past her, and another memory overtook her: on the night she spent hiding in Eugene's closet, she had heard a woman sigh. *The blonde swimmer. In Eugene's bed, but gone by morning. That girl had been no truer to Gilbert Howard than he had been to her. No truer than Eugene's word to me.*

She walked back along the path again, this time toward the front door of her own Villa 7B. She knew the police might still be there, although she would surely have noticed lights and movement inside. But they might be waiting for her. It was, she supposed, one of those moments when a criminal, after planning everything perfectly, makes a blunder that breaks the case wide open. She was not a criminal, but she could blunder with the best of them. She had to, now that she had lost her ring. There was nothing for it but to see for herself whether her forty dollars were really missing from the sofa cushions, for it was entirely possible that Eugene had lied about looking for the money, too.

Villa 7B appeared to be perfectly empty. Once inside the front room, Frankie didn't turn on the light—she was not so foolish as that. In darkness she made her way to the sofa. She set the cushions on the floor, thrust her fingers deeply into the crease at the back and into the corners, and sat back on her heels, empty-handed. Her money was not there. What to search next—kitchen, bedroom, or bath?

She entered the unlit bedroom and stopped still. On Connie's bed she made out a black shape stretched out asleep. Connie was back. Frankie stepped up to shake her awake and ask her where the money was. Her brogue found something slippery on the floor by the bed and she barely managed to catch her balance.

She put out a hand and found the little frilled lamp by the bedside. She switched it on.

Once the light clicked on, she saw her error.

The Queen of the Extras lay unmoving in Connie's bed. Frankie couldn't think why. Had Loretta hoped to help Frankie somehow, or had she come by to console, comfort, and reassure her? Frankie leaned closer.

The dark hair at the near side of the Queen's head shone with blood.

Somebody had struck her on the head and killed her. The Queen was dead.

"Oh, my Queen." Frankie switched off the light. She sat down on the side of the bed and buried her face in her hands. First Gilbert Howard, and now the Queen. Mother to all at Paradise Gardens. Almost a mother to Frankie herself.

Across the dark little room, Frankie heard a rustle. It was the sort of sound that a person might make who had been sitting out of sight on the floor and was now finding his or her feet. *Hers.* Frankie heard a soft footstep—a woman's step. She was sure of it.

There was no sense trying to hide. There was nowhere *to* hide. She reached over the Queen's body and switched the light on again.

There at the foot of the bed stood the Hollywood columnist, Blanche Carver.

"I knew Gilbert Howard's killer would return to the scene of the crime," Blanche Carver said. "But I never guessed that you'd kill my poor dear Loretta, too."

CHAPTER TWO

Frankie knelt in the pool of light by Connie's bed, where the Queen lay, her poor head resting on the bloodied pillow. "Dear Queen, dear Loretta, who will look after us now?"

From behind Frankie, near the bedroom door, Blanche spoke again. "I know who you are. In disguise! I heard a woman's voice in the dark, but I see a man when I turn on the light. We've met before, and more than once, *Francesca Ray*."

With gentle fingers, Frankie touched the Queen's hair. "How long has she been lying here? How long have you known she was dead?"

"Not long. My poor Loretta." The columnist shook her head. "The police will be here soon to take you into custody. And then I'm going to print the hardest story I've ever had to write. The whole world will know what you did to the woman who welcomed and helped you."

Frankie faced Blanche. No wonder the columnist hadn't shown up at Camillo's, looking for gossip and scoops. She had been sitting beside the Queen's body, keeping vigil with her friend.

Frankie said, "I didn't do this. I would never hurt her."

"Lies. Every one of them takes you one step closer to trial, jail, and execution."

Frankie bent over the Queen again. She wanted to make sure that the dead woman's eyes were shut, not open like poor Gilbert Howard's had been. But the Queen's eyes were closed and she looked as if she were sleeping, which was how Frankie had always expected a dead person to look. In fact, the Queen, tucked up into Connie's bed with her head on the pillow, appeared to be simply resting her eyes after a day's hard work, if you didn't take into account the bloodstains on the pillowcase.

Frankie looked up at Blanche. The columnist held something in her right hand. A bag? A stick? It didn't matter.

"She's been hit on the head," Frankie said.

"Not exactly news to you, is it?"

Frankie grimaced but held back her retort. She said evenly, "The police were posted all around this villa after Gilbert Howard was found here. Why weren't they here to save her?"

"The police found evidence that Howie was murdered in his own bungalow, and the body merely transported to yours. They moved their investigation away from Paradise Gardens, next door to the Garden of Allah."

"If only they had left a policeman here." Frankie felt her throat grow thick with tears, but she wouldn't cry. How much better to recite poetry, as Billie had done over Gilbert Howard's body. For once, she couldn't recall a single verse of the Bible, nor a word of Shakespeare, except for *Alas.*

So she said that. "Alas, dear Queen."

"Alas, indeed, for Loretta." Blanche held up the item she'd been cradling against her breast. Frankie saw that it was the lamp from her own bedside table — like Connie's, minus its ruffled shade. The columnist's expression was fierce, as if she were going to strike out with it.

"Miss Carver, what are you doing with my lamp?"

"This was the murder weapon, wasn't it?"

"Was it?" Frankie stared. The columnist must be correct. Except for its twin still sitting on Connie's bedside table, this wrought-iron lamp was the only object in the room that might serve as a weapon. She leaned closer to look at the Queen's head wound in the light from Connie's lamp. She tipped back the frilly shade to examine the back of the Queen's head more closely.

"It looks like she was hit from behind."

"I'm remembering every word you say," Blanche said. "It's only fair to tell you. Each remark that you make will be printed in my paper and then, later on, revealed in court."

The columnist took a step closer to the side of the bed opposite Frankie.

Frankie clasped her hands in front of her, the way her father had taught her to stand during a church service. She said, "My Queen, on behalf of all of your kids at Paradise Gardens, thank you. I believe that all the good that you've done, all the help you've given, will come back to you, somehow, wherever you are now. Go in peace."

"It's practically a confession." Blanche held the lamp to her breast.

Frankie leaned over to kiss the Queen's cheek, almost as pale as the pillowcase beneath her head. The cheek was still warm. That meant that she had arrived only moments too late to stop whomever had done this terrible thing. If only she hadn't hung about, talking to Eugene, chasing after the blonde girl who was, all the time, hiding in Eugene's house.

Had Eugene attacked the Queen? But why would he? That thought sent the mystery spiralling even deeper than before. Because there was no getting around it. A second dead body in Villa 7B meant only one thing: the Queen had been killed because of Gilbert Howard. But by whom? Perhaps the Queen had found Gilbert Howard's blonde swimmer and communicated Frankie's suspicions to the girl herself.

Frankie leaned over the Queen's body and touched her hand. It was neutral to the touch, no colder than Frankie's own hand. Frankie started, put two fingers under the Queen's chin at the side of the neck, and looked sharply up at Blanche.

"She's not dead." Frankie was conscious of her own heart beating hard within her breast. "The Queen is alive."

"I felt for Loretta's pulse before you came." Blanche stood. She dropped the lamp onto the end of the bed. A smear of blood stained her white jacket. "She had none."

"Her pulse is faint, but it's there."

"I must have missed it. Thank God," Blanche whispered. "Now, what should we do?"

"*What should we do?* Great heavens." Frankie took the gun out of her pocket. "We should call a doctor! Get out of my way, Miss Carver."

Frankie yanked the door open, half expecting to receive a wrought-iron lamp on the back of her head, courtesy of the columnist. She sprinted into the brick patio area where she had lately danced the carioca with Eugene. She placed two fingers into the trigger loop, pointed King Samson's gun straight up in the air, peered into the darkness to see that the sky was empty of birds directly overhead, closed her eyes, and pulled the trigger.

Nothing happened—the trigger was stuck on something. She peered at the gun in the darkness, and saw a glint of light on the trigger, like a tiny star caught on a small new moon. Here it was after all: the engagement ring that Champ had given her that day in the snow. Her ring had hooked itself onto the trigger. With excruciating delicacy of movement, she wiggled it free and dropped the ring into her jacket pocket. She pointed the gun straight up and fired.

The gun went off with a sound like the end of the world. Frankie shouted for help. Then she aimed, checked again, and pulled the trigger.

The gun cracked again, but the Paradise Gardens kids were already running along pathways and out of bungalow doors toward her, some in bathrobes, some in bare feet. A nursery rhyme sounded in Frankie's head. *Leave your supper and leave your sleep. Come to your playfellows in the street.* She wished she were calling them to meet in a long conga line, to dance through the night.

Her chattering, friendly young neighbours gathered around Frankie. Eugene was among them — quieter, as always, than most — but the golden girl was nowhere to be seen. She spotted Tom's blue sweater in the crush of young people, took a handful of his sleeve, and pressed her face to his ear. Briefly, she filled him in on the Queen's situation.

"Got it," Tom said. "Thank goodness you found her. We'll get her to hospital, Frankie."

She jumped as if shot. "You know who I *am?*"

"*Frank Achilles*, of course. The Queen told me all about your disguise." Tom looked sharply at Frankie. "Did you think any one of us would turn you in, Frankie? The Queen trusts us."

Frankie exhaled. "I trust you, too. Let's get the Queen to hospital." But how they would carry the injured woman without harming her further, Frankie didn't know. She found that she didn't know anything at all, except that Eugene Ellery was the first through the door into Villa 7B. He carried one corner of the Queen's mattress. The mattress was too thin to behave like a proper stretcher, but with so many hands, the crowd of young people managed to keep the Queen something near to horizontal as they carried her out toward Sunset Boulevard. Tom picked up the corner of the chenille counterpane where it dragged on the bricks and tucked it safely out of the way. He handed off his spot at the side of the mattress to somebody else. "Frankie, we were all hoping you'd be halfway to Canada by now. The cops haven't come up with a single alternate suspect yet, which makes us wonder what they use for brains."

"I know," Frankie said, breathing hard. "They stopped me on the street a couple of times. They asked me to identify my own picture."

Somehow the sound of Tom's laugh made Frankie certain that the Queen would survive her attacker's blow. Tom said, "We'll take care of the Queen. Leave her to us. Make your escape before the police and the press find out you're disguised as a man, will you?"

He followed the rest out toward Sunset.

The press, of course, in the shape of Blanche Carver, already knew Frankie was disguised as Frank Achilles. But she couldn't do anything about Blanche Carver just then. She did, however, know at last where to find the golden swimmer. She plunged up the path and through Villa 7A's unlocked front door. Gun in hand, she burst inside Eugene's bathroom, but it was empty. She pounded through his house — tore the back of his cupboard open and checked under the bed, but found no golden swimmer anywhere. The blonde girl was gone again.

Frankie walked slowly out of doors. If Blanche Carver had called the police as she'd said, they would be here any moment now. If this were to be the end of the road for Frank Achilles — and for Frankie Ray — she had better savour her last experience of freedom in Hollywood.

She gazed up into unfathomable California sky and told it, "I shouldn't have run in the first place. There was nothing to tie me to Gilbert Howard's murder except its location. I hardly knew him. I was never his lover, and the kids and the Queen of Paradise Gardens would have testified so. But I ran." What dreadful moments those had been, lightened only by the friendship and protection she had felt when Eugene Ellery took her and hid her. *The same way Eugene had sheltered the blonde swimmer.* "And now I'm the only suspect in a front-page murder investigation. But anyway, I won't run now."

Around her, the shrubs and hedges whispered. The stars stared down at her. She caught a glimpse of a pale face like a flash of moonlight at the door of Villa 7B.

Blanche Carver spoke from the bungalow's doorway. "You had a gun all the time."

Frankie put her hand in her pocket and left it there, resting on the gun. Yes, this gun had been with her that first night in Vancouver, when the adventure had begun. It had been with her the whole time, in fact, with the exception of the few hours during which somebody had used it to shoot Gilbert Howard. She almost laughed as she said, "Yes, I'm armed to the teeth."

"But you didn't use it? Why not, when you could have held me up and made your escape?"

Impatiently, Frankie shook her head. "Go ahead and print what I said: *I should never have run.* I should have shown better sense, but when you accused me of the murder, I was afraid."

Blanche took a few steps nearer Frankie. "You had a gun, but you were afraid?"

"I didn't have the gun when I found Gilbert Howard's body. But I would have been afraid even if I had."

A siren sounded not far off, and Frankie's shoulders tensed under her man's jacket. But the siren drifted away into the distance.

She asked, "Where are the policemen, Miss Carver? If you called them, shouldn't they be here by now?"

The columnist stopped, her white trouser suit glowing in the darkness. She opened her mouth as if to answer, but said nothing.

Understanding rose in Frankie like a great, round, illuminating moon. She said, "It's a mystery, isn't it, when you phone the police about a murder—even an attempted murder—and they don't show up. It's as if you hadn't even called in the first place. Perhaps you wanted the story all to yourself?"

Blanche Carver said nothing.

"But that's not it at all, is it, Miss Carver? Because an even stranger puzzle can be found in the geometry of the scene. The geometry that, according to you, had me hit the Queen with a lamp, escape and then stupidly return to be caught by you, my accuser."

As if she hadn't heard a word Frankie had said, Blanche asked, "Do you think Loretta will be all right?"

"I don't know. How hard did you hit her?"

Frankie took out the gun again. She had a deep wish to say *an eye for an eye, a tooth for a tooth.* She wanted to rage against liars and bearers of false witness. She wanted to frighten the life out of the woman and then lead her at gunpoint to the police station.

Instead, she fired the gun twice more into the evening sky. Paradise Gardens was empty, and the night seemed undisturbed by the noise. Nobody came running. You'd think that the police next door in the Garden of Allah, at Gilbert Howard's bungalow, would hear and investigate a noise like that. But maybe they were slower on their feet than when you saw them in the movies.

"I wanted to empty the gun," Frankie explained. She slipped it back into her pocket. "Ammunition is really far too much of a temptation."

"I'll deny this if you tell anybody," Blanche Carver said, "but I thought Loretta was *you*. You had escaped the night before, and the police had finished with the scene and left. I was alone in your room, in the dark, trying to get a feel for the moment an aspiring actress becomes a murderess. I was trying to imagine how you killed my friend Gilbert Howard. Then I heard movement in the living room. The door opened. I thought you had returned to the scene of the crime. I knew you were armed and dangerous, so I took the lamp and I … I hit Loretta by accident," Blanche Carver said reasonably. "I wouldn't hurt a friend on purpose. And they couldn't … I mean, as a murderer, you couldn't be …"

Frankie finished her sentence for her. "They couldn't execute me twice for two murders, so I might as well take the blame." Would the world agree? If so, what a heartless world this was. She kicked a stone off the patio onto the grass in front of Villa 7B. "Two murders for the price of one. How thrifty. Well, Miss Carver, tell me this. You hurt the Queen. Hurt her badly. So I have to ask you, *did you kill Gilbert Howard?*"

Blanche said, "Don't be silly. He was my friend."

"Like Loretta—the Queen—was your friend?"

"I've known her all my life."

"I have a friend like that." Or she used to have, before their definitive quarrel. "Miss Carver, you need to decide what to do about me now. Call the police if you must. I can't stop you now that I've emptied my gun."

The columnist nodded. "You might have shot me, but you didn't. You could have run, but you chose to stay and see that Loretta got help." Blanche Carver pierced Frankie with her sharp newspaperwoman's gaze. "You know something? I don't think you killed Gilbert Howard at all. So I'd better give you a good long start, hadn't I?"

Blanche Carver walked past Frankie toward Sunset. Over her shoulder she said, "I'll keep your disguise to myself. There."

"If you're hoping I'll say thank you, Miss Carver, you're in for a long wait."

Blanche Carver's white form vanished round a corner. Frankie tried to feel angry with the woman, but she felt hungry instead — desperately so. Untimely so! That lobster dinner at Camillo's seemed a long time ago. Luckily, there was food in Villa 7B's kitchenette. From the kitchen cupboard she snatched the half-empty bag of bread that had provided her and Connie with such pleasant toast the morning before. She stepped out the back door and peered through the darkness into the branches of the famously productive orange tree, in hopes of finding some fruit to sweeten her plain bread supper. But she forgot all about oranges at the sound of a deep sigh. Turning, she spied the starlit the figure of a woman kneeling in the grass in Eugene's backyard.

Almost at once she made out that the woman on the grass was not the golden swimmer. This woman's hair was dark, and she was bent over as if crying, as if she were a mourner. And she was kneeling over the spot where Frankie had helped Eugene uncover the 'anonymous' dead man. Frankie was certain there had never been two dead bodies in one day at Villa 7B. The backyard corpse and Gilbert Howard had been one and the same. While she and Connie had been extras in the movies, somebody had dug up Gilbert Howard's body and posed it on the sofa in Frankie's living room.

Frankie watched from the shadow beneath the orange tree as the weeping woman rose to her feet. Frankie saw first that she was barefoot, and second that she was Marietta Valdes. The actress picked up two objects that Frankie had not previously noticed: two buckets, one for each hand. She strode away, as all the world was doing tonight, toward Sunset Boulevard.

It occurred to Frankie that if Marietta Valdes had known where to kneel in Eugene's backyard to cry over Gilbert Howard's death, then it followed that she might very well know who had buried him there.

Frankie took three pieces of bread from the bag and dropped the rest against the base of the orange tree. Munching on bits of dry bread, she followed Marietta, staying out of the light and trying not to slap the soles of her brogues on the path between the bungalows.

She was back out on Sunset Boulevard, trailing Marietta at a conservative distance, before she realized that somebody was trailing *her*.

A line from the 'Rubaiyat of Omar Khayyam' came to mind. Her father Sheridan D had never approved of the poem. He thought it too sensual, and so Frankie had learned several bits of it by heart. She had been struck by the truth of one line among many: *The Moving Finger writes, and having writ, moves on.* You couldn't take back a lie once you'd spoken it.

Right now Frankie was sincerely glad that she had lied to Blanche Carver and left a single bullet in the gun.

CHAPTER THREE

A soft wind lifted and rattled the palm fronds as Marietta, followed by Frankie, who was trailed in her turn by a shadowy, unknown pursuer, walked swiftly along Sunset Boulevard.

Marietta certainly had tough feet. She covered ground with a speed remarkable for a barefoot woman carrying two buckets. What on earth was Marietta Valdes carrying in those buckets? Water? Why on earth would she be carrying a couple of gallons of water alone at night on Sunset Boulevard? At any rate, it was apparent that she was a walker. Connie's mother was a walker, too, Frankie recalled. Mrs Mooney was as round as a doughnut, but she could roll on forever once she started. And of course, Frankie's own mother had been very good at walking away.

The three of them, still keeping a neat distance one from the next, neared Monument Studios. Frankie became aware of a new sound, a distant hiss and pop. It sounded like the fireworks she and Connie used to buy with their pocket money every autumn. To match the two noises properly, you'd have to add the hiss of sparklers to the pop of the firecrackers.

Fire. Now Frankie remembered, for the Queen had told her the day before about King Samson's planned great conflagration, when he would burn the decade-old set for his epic *Ambition.*

Earlier this very evening, Connie had been enthusing about going to the filming of the fire. She would have discovered the impossibility of entering the studio without a pass by now, Frankie supposed.

But Marietta must have a pass, or be named on a list, for the actress moved confidently across the street to the Monument Studio gates, past Dickie the guard's kiosk, and up to the small door set into the larger gates. The actress put down her buckets and pounded on the door.

Frankie stood behind a fat palm trunk to watch. High above, a puff of white smoke rose into the night, and Frankie wondered what would happen if the wind blew harder and swept the fire beyond the studio walls. No wonder Dickie's kiosk was empty. All hands, and no doubt a lot of firemen, would be on the far side of the studios, standing guard as the set of *Ambition* burned.

Between keeping an eye on Marietta hammering at the gate and the rising clouds of smoke, Frankie completely missed the sound of footsteps coming up behind until they were right upon her. A hand touched her shoulder.

A voice said quietly, "Did you decide that you couldn't leave Hollywood without seeing the show, Frankie?"

Eugene. This was the first time she'd been so near him since she'd uncovered his lie about not finding the golden swimmer. And she had not forgotten that she was in this mess in the first place because he'd urged her to evade the law. But he was still Eugene Ellery, the man with the calm and helpful grey eyes. And—perhaps because of her appreciation of his slight frame and elegant attire, and the way his jacket was always buttoned, with the tie perfectly tied in a Prince Albert knot—she still wanted to trust Eugene. It occurred to her that perhaps love was not a storm or a blessing or even a journey. It might simply be a choice you were driven by circumstances to make.

Frankie murmured calmly, "Oh! When you say 'watch the show', do you mean to watch the *Ambition* set burn down? I understand that the fire will be fearfully controlled."

"King Samson has fifty engineers on hand to help, I hear," Eugene said.

"So Connie told me." Frankie said, "Somebody told me that King Samson's got a team of firemen, too, and air pipes to make the flames climb higher while the cameramen film the blaze."

"No expense spared, the papers say."

"Naturally. It's King Samson." Frankie inclined her head. "Burning *Ambition*."

"What a well-turned phrase," Eugene said. "*And* you know how to dance the carioca. My, you're a clever young woman, Frankie."

She looked away from him, straight ahead at the angels guarding Monument Studios. She asked, "Do you love her?"

"Love who?" Eugene asked.

Before Frankie could answer, the gate to the studios was flung open from within. Marietta picked up her buckets and disappeared inside. The gate banged shut again, but Frankie made out the thin black upright line along the doorframe that told her the force of its closing had bounced it open again.

"Do you love the blonde girl?" she clarified.

"What blonde girl?" Eugene frowned.

Frankie walked away from him toward the studio door. Over her shoulder she added, "The blonde girl who was naked in your bathroom."

She certainly hoped that would leave him speechless — stop him short, in fact, while she strode across the street and left him behind.

He caught up to her. She found herself a little closer to Eugene than she wanted to be at that particular time and place.

"No," he said. "I don't love the blonde girl. I guess I don't even like her very much." He drew breath. "Frankie, go home to your father. Be safe. Be yourself again."

With a fierce tug Frankie freed her arm from his grip, gave him a minister's Judgement-Day look, and strode through the studio door. She knew he'd follow her. Or perhaps she hoped he'd follow her. But she didn't look back.

Once inside the studio gates, she looked to her left at the offices where Frank Achilles had so recently been given the star treatment. Only a couple of lights glowed in the office windows. Tonight, King Samson and all his employees would be at the fire. Here within the studio walls, the crackle of the fire sounded very close indeed, but she was certain it was well under control. There would be laws about that in Hollywood, or at least guidelines to be followed for the insurance companies.

The sounds the fire made, and the chemical smell it produced—an odour that she had no name for—excited her and hurried her steps along the same path she'd taken two days before, when the Queen had guided her and Connie among the sound stages to join the extras. Between the buildings she caught sight of the black-painted pillar topped with the head of the dog-faced Egyptian god Anubis. Its ears gleamed orange and gold from the flames that must soon catch up with it and burn it to the ground.

She rounded the corner of a sound stage and found herself in the open, gravelly area where she had met Bruno and the other extras. Was it only yesterday that they had gathered to smoke, drink coffee, and eat cheese and tomato sandwiches while waiting to be filmed? Tonight in the gloom, the litter of paper cups and cigarette butts shone like pearls against the ground. She remembered the extras' friendly banter, and the moment she had been chosen, against all the odds, for the role of pigeon girl. Despite all the darkness, unfairness, and danger the time between had brought, Frankie felt herself smile from ear to ear.

Eugene's steps rattled the gravel behind her. She snapped back to the present moment and hurried away from him, around the corner and onto the pigeon-girl set.

Beyond the statue of the horse with three feet on the ground stood the wall separating the pigeon-girl movie set from the old set of *Ambition*. A tongue of flames beyond this inner wall licked upward, and Frankie saw Marietta's two buckets resting on the gravel nearby. Marietta herself appeared out of a gap in the set wall, moving quickly in her swirling red dress. There was no sign on her angry, beautiful face that she'd been crying twenty minutes before. She looked like a goddess who'd never shed a tear in her life. Behind her, Luigi dragged a camera on wheels across the gravel. Marietta cursed him soundly over her shoulder, and the cameraman cursed back in Italian.

Eugene called, "Marietta! What lunatic scheme are you devising now?"

Marietta's eyes flashed as she turned from Luigi and his camera to face them. "Eugene! And Frank Achilles. Excellent. Please explain to this cameraman that a great film does not simply survive the plots and machinations of writers, cameramen, and engineers. Every inch of film must spring whole from the mind of a director, like Athena from the brow of Zeus."

"*Strega!*" the cameraman blazed at Marietta. "I know *everything* about directing. I agree, don't listen to the producer. And don't listen to the bloody actors. Above all, don't listen to the writers. But if you want a picture, you'd better damn well listen to your cameraman — me! — and also the one who let you in through the gate."

"You took my money, Luigi. You'll stay and shoot film as I say," Marietta told him coolly, "on *this* side of the wall, where I control the filming. Exactly as if I were the director of *The Emperor of New York*. Because that's what I'm going to be. Here, hold these matches."

Marietta tossed a box of matches to Luigi. Then she snatched up one of her buckets and swung it back.

Frankie cried, "Don't empty it!"

There was a frozen moment when the bucket hung horizontally as if defying gravity — and then its contents flew straight out in front of Marietta. The slosh of liquid spread across the façade of the columned building set, the one that had the look of a bank. She said, "That's liquid paraffin. Light it and film the results, Luigi. And don't overlook the visual ratio. The perfect rectangular shot! No burning obelisk can compete with a flaming colonnade."

Luigi looked doubtfully from the matchbox to the paraffin-glazed colonnade.

"How can you hope to control a fire without a team of engineers?" Frankie demanded.

"Damn the engineers." Marietta picked up the second bucket.

Frankie moved to stop her, but Eugene pushed Frankie aside and attempted to wrestle the second bucket away from her. Frankie heard the splash of spilled liquid. A shining string of dots shone like a small cluster of stars as some of the contents splashed across the arm and side of Eugene's jacket.

"Look out!" Frankie cried.

Eugene, still struggling with the actress for the second bucket, said, "Marietta, if you light this part of the set on fire without the engineers to control it, the fire may spread. The whole of Sunset Boulevard could go up in flames."

"Don't be a coward. Art is everything." Marietta won the struggle and slung the bucket's contents onto the set building so that the columns looked like a bit of Atlantis pulled up from the bottom of the sea. "Look behind you—see those big drums? Water. Water in case of fire. *I* had those set there for safety's sake. You see? I've thought it through."

Marietta might have been more convincing had she not, to Frankie's certain knowledge, been drinking quite a lot of champagne at Camillo's earlier that night. The two enormous cans of water were better than nothing, but they were no substitute for trained firefighters.

As if on cue, excited voices sounded from the far side of the old *Ambition* set wall. Out of Frankie's sight, firemen and engineers rattled off numbers, reports, and orders.

"Twenty-seven's on the line."

"Eighteen's a go."

"Nineteen's stuck. Give me a hand, will you?"

"Stand by with the hoses."

It was a comfort to know that, not far off, King Samson and all his brave firemen and engineers were standing by to handle the burning of *Ambition*.

Eugene gestured emphatically toward the columned building Marietta had drenched in paraffin. "What if you light this wall and it burns out of control? What if you kill somebody, Marietta?"

"Then I'll film it. Light the fire, Luigi, you lily-livered slave." Marietta snatched the matches from his hands.

Luigi roared, "*Ammaliatrice!* Go to hell and take your paraffin with you."

"That particular road runs both ways, Luigi, and don't you forget it." In a passion, Marietta flung out both arms. Her right hand, which held the matches, missed Frankie's left eye by a narrow margin.

"Ha!" Frankie cried and seized the matches from Marietta.

Marietta lunged and attempted to take them back, but Frankie slipped the matches safely into her pocket with the gun.

When Marietta drew back a fist, Eugene stepped between them and took hold of the actress by both wrists.

"You're both against me. You don't want me to become a director any more than King Samson does." Marietta grew calm Eugene's grip. "But you'll see. I'll find myself some fire on the far side of this wall. I'll get my shots in there. Come on, Luigi. Unless you want to pay back all that money I gave you."

Marietta pulled free of Eugene and strode away through the gap in the firewall. Luigi followed her, grumbling and tugging his wheeled camera behind him. Frankie let out a long breath.

"Thank goodness." Eugene flung himself down on the plinth at the foot of the statue.

"Nobody could really like Marietta Valdes." Frankie eyed the columns and classical portico that topped them, all drenched in unlit liquid paraffin. "But I hope she does become Hollywood's first woman director. I do."

"I like Marietta fine. When she's not acting crazy," Eugene said. "Still, it would surprise me very much if she got the chance to direct." He added, "Except maybe a short film. I hear that a woman on Goldwyn's lot is directing short films."

Frankie shoved her hand into her pocket. She touched the gun, the ring, and the box of matches. She was very glad indeed that she'd taken the matches from Marietta, for the pigeon-girl set was at least safe.

A series of bangs sounded on the far side of the *Ambition* set firewall. The night breeze picked up, and something metallic popped loudly, out of sight. Standing side by side in the centre of the pigeon-girl set, Frankie and Eugene were perfectly placed to witness a long, slender arc of flame rise like a finger and top the firewall. The flame tip licked at the colonnaded bank façade Marietta had so recently drenched with flammable liquid. The actress's wish had come true. Along with the *Ambition* set, the pigeon-girl set was on fire.

Eugene leapt to his feet. Frankie gaped as the bottom of one of the columns caught with a liquid crackle. Flames sprouted across the set's façade like a magical golden vine. Eugene ran up to the burning façade, apparently forgetting that his jacket sleeve was wet with paraffin.

"That jacket's not safe." Frankie charged up beside him. "Take it off before it catches fire."

Eugene looked down at his jacket. "I'll keep it on."

And then, loud enough to be heard above the popping of the fire, the hissing of gas, and the faint bellows from the firefighters and engineers, Frankie heard a scream. It came from the far side of the firewall, and for a second she believed that the scream was part of the filming, acted out for the cameras on *Ambition's* burning set. But only for that brief moment.

She knew that scream. She had heard it brought out at

intervals by grade-school tumbles in the schoolyard and, more often, by adolescent frustrations. She knew the author of the scream well enough to hear the genuine panic.

She said, "It's Connie. Connie's in the fire."

Eugene said, "Dear lord. Stay calm, Frankie. Samson's army of engineers can't be far off. I'll go find them."

Frankie didn't answer him. She didn't need an expert knowledge of fire to know that flames moved quickly once they'd taken hold. The opening in the firewall would take her to Connie. Head down, she tore toward it.

"Frankie, *wait*."

"I can't."

"You must." He ran up behind her and took hold of her arm. "Listen. Take a moment to soak your jacket in Marietta's water drums. That way you can wrap the heavy cloth around your face if you run into smoke. Like this." He removed his suit jacket, and she tore her own jacket off and plunged it into the water drum with his. "I'm coming in with you," he added.

"Thank you, Eugene." Frankie hauled her jacket, dripping, out of the water. On second thought, she picked up one of the smaller buckets, swooshed it clean of paraffin, and filled it with water. She dumped it over Eugene's head and then her own, soaking their shirts and trousers. The stream blinded her for a moment as her hair, short as it was, plastered itself over her eyes. Frankie shoved it back with her father's second-best oath. She glanced down at herself. The water on her white men's shirt made the Xeno-Flex Combination show through, the lace trim around the neck marking it clearly and unmistakably as a woman's undergarment. But there was no time to worry about that. Anyway, Eugene already knew she was a woman.

She sped after him. He accelerated toward the gap in the firewall. Smoke poured through the opening in the wall now, so she held the wet sleeve of her coat to her face before passing through. Once inside, she peered around, looking for Eugene among the timbered, Egyptian-style wooden pieces standing almost obscured by smoke but as yet untouched by the fire.

She moved toward the sound of the fire, in the direction Connie's call had come from. Ahead of her she saw the reflection of flames on painted wood.

She put a hand to the firewall on her right. It was nearly hot enough to blister her palm. She stumbled over a pipe running across her path and knocked over a bucket of something she hoped to heaven was water. Connie was nowhere to be seen. Frankie called out Connie's name and then Eugene's, but heard no answer over the crack and sibilance of the fire. An urgent desire to run back the way she'd come overtook her. She hoped that the former Reverend Sheridan D Ray hadn't raised a coward.

She called out to Connie and soldiered on, moving deeper among the smoking panels and the reverse sides of building facades, glad of her tough men's brogues on the uneven terrain. How was it that men in paintings and poetry appeared so brave, striding into battle to protect country and hearth with their shoulders squared and jaws set? Perhaps their boldness was a disguise, like Frankie's brogues, haircut, and Xeno-Flex Combination. Maybe inside themselves, men felt like Frankie did now: scared to death.

She coughed to clear her throat and shouted Connie's name. On her right, the firewall split, and one side yawned toward her. She slipped through the V-shaped gap in the *Ambition* set, ducking out of the way of falling sparks and bits of glowing wood. From atop a slender pillar, the dog-faced god Anubis stared down at her. A little farther off she made out the tail end of a sphinx, its curved hips lit by flames that consumed its face.

Running footsteps sounded behind her, and Frankie looked back through the gap in the firewall. A cry of wonder and relief escaped her, for on the other side Eugene was staggering by the opening. His arm supported Connie, and his bunched-up jacket half-covered Connie's face. Connie wore the white dress from Camillo's, now fringed in grubby grey. Eugene's shirt clung damply to his torso.

At the sight of that torso, revealed like her own Xeno-Flex Combination through wet shirting, Frankie was struck speechless. She gaped after Connie and Eugene, coughing into the wet sleeve of her jacket.

She struggled to grasp Eugene's secret.

Her delay proved an instant too long. Behind her, flames took hold of the pedestal at the base of the dog-faced statue. She heard the crack of breaking wood. She looked up at the falling shadow.

Darkness struck her and knocked her to the ground.

Chapter Four

Frankie woke herself, coughing. Above her, the night sky was greyed with smoke. Around her, tattered, grimy bits of wall bore painted Egyptian symbols. From somewhere nearby she heard the crackle and scuttle of flames in the old wooden movie sets. The pillar that had held aloft the dog-faced god Anubis lay fallen across her legs. She could feel the pressure of it, but most of its weight rested on jumbled bits of set. She tried to push herself free but could not. She pushed at the pillar, but it wouldn't move. It was wet and oily, and she couldn't get purchase with her hands to move it or herself. She twisted one way and the other, and then both ways at once.

She slammed both palms hard against the pillar. The pain helped her focus on the geometrical problem she faced. She saw it as if it were drawn in chalk on a classroom blackboard. On the other side of the pillar, out of sight, her left leg was trapped and contorted by a smaller obstacle of some kind. If her geometry was correct, that obstacle lay across the farthest edge of the pillar that spanned and immobilized her legs and hips. Her left leg was the key. If she could get that one loose, the rest of her ought to follow. She wriggled and angled, an inch this way and an iota that.

She reminded herself that she was not alone on the burning set of *Ambition*. Firemen and engineers would be nearby, controlling the fire. Cameramen would be roaming about, seeking memorable shots. Somebody would surely find her.

As the flames approached, Frankie pulled her damp shirt across her nose and mouth and made three impossible wishes.

First, that she had never come to Hollywood.

Second, that for once in her life Connie would apologize for getting her into this situation.

Third, Frankie wished with all her heart that she had said a proper goodbye to her poor father, who would be devastated when he heard that she had perished in a movie-set fire. *Dad, they'll say I killed a movie star. They'll say I shot him. Don't believe a word of it. If only I could move, I'd get out of here and find out who really killed Gilbert Howard.*

She relived the shock she'd felt when she saw Eugene fleeing the fire with Connie. For it was then that Frankie had seen, through Eugene's soaked shirting, small but entirely female breasts.

Like Frankie, Eugene was a woman dressed as a man. Frankie was so mad at herself for not realizing the truth, and at Eugene for lying, that she regained a little more of her natural can-do spirit.

She struggled. She called. She rested.

And then she learned that when danger had you cornered and pinned down, you weren't alone after all. It was like when you were a little child and felt afraid. You'd call out in the darkness. One of your parents would come to you, sit down on the edge of your bed, and lay a hand on your shoulder. Your mother would say, *Close your eyes and go to sleep.* Your father would murmur, *That's my brave Frankie.* And the door would stand marginally open to brighten the night with a yellow slice of the adult world. What a surprise it was to find that, a thousand miles away, those gestures of comfort remained with her from so long ago, from even before memories began. Here in the middle of the smoke and danger, Frankie saw both her parents quite clearly, her mother on her left and her father on her right. She felt encouraged by their presence and tried again to wriggle herself free. And she prayed that they would stay — that they would not leave her alone with the fire.

Her struggles grew weaker.

She redoubled her attempts.

She rested again. The smoke was so thick that she was having trouble breathing, and she was well beyond speaking. But her mother urged her to hold on, and Sheridan D, with his great minister's voice, called for help.

Chapter Five

Somewhere among the smoke and shadows of the burning *Ambition* set, a woman was laughing. The laughter sounded too harsh and cawing for Heaven, so Frankie guessed she was still alive. She had no idea how long she had been lying here, nor how late the night had grown.

One of her trapped legs was numb. Heat licked the left side of her face. She heard a rumbling, like a tumble of logs on the beach. A woman—the same woman who had been laughing?—swore. Without any more warning than that, Frankie's legs came free of the pillar that had trapped her. She fell onto her side. Coughing, and weak with disbelief, she looked up into Marietta Valdes's inquisitive gaze.

The actress's face glowed in reflected light from the fire—the same fire that appeared to be eating the nearby sphinx whole. More dangerously still, the flames were chewing the end of the tumbled-down column of the dog-faced god. Marietta couldn't have moved that pillar by herself. Even she, so capable and brilliant, must have had a man's help with this at least.

But whoever her other rescuer had been—fire-fighter? engineer? cameraman?—Marietta and Frankie were on their own now. Two women trapped in a fire! But she remembered that neither Marietta nor her other rescuer knew that Frankie was not really a man, and anyway the heaviest work was done.

Frankie was free. And now Marietta had an arm under Frankie's shoulder and was attempting to hoist her upright. Frankie coughed and lost her footing, pins and needles hot as fire in the leg that was asleep.

Marietta grunted, "Frank Achilles, old fellow, do you think you might try to help a little?"

Frankie did her best. The two of them stumbled over a dislodged chunk of rock on the uneven ground, and Marietta hauled them upright again, stumbling away from the fire, talking all the time. "A fire is wonderful theatre. Storytelling is transformation."

Frankie croaked, "It nearly transformed me, all right."

"Exactly. That's what fire does — causes a *metamorphosis* — and that's why it's so important to get the angles. As many as you can! And every angle of interception and direction has to be different. Every single angle must be so unrecognizable from the last that the audience senses itself riding helter-skelter into the unknown."

"Abso-tively."

They staggered alongside the smoky set wall, through a hole in a firewall, and burst out onto the pigeon-girl set. There, the fire Marietta had started with her buckets of paraffin oil had burned out.

"Well done, Frank Achilles." Marietta slapped her hands together. "Here we are. Safe as houses."

"Thank all the heavens for that — and thank you, Marietta." Frankie hefted her suit jacket. Her jacket pockets felt awfully light. Unweighted.

Somehow, she had lost the gun. She pictured the weapon lying amid the smoking rubble. In her imagination, it went up with a bang. But, in all the conflagration, what would one more explosion matter?

A small group of firemen emerged through the same opening in the wall. Black helmets shining, rubberized coats unbuttoned down the front, the men huddled together, lighting cigarettes and laughing in the darkness. Smoke drifted by, following the light wind.

To the right of the horse statue, three more firemen kicked at the last bits of the charred ruin of the colonnaded bank. On Frankie's left, Luigi the cameraman crouched at the foot of his wheeled camera, sorting through small, black tins of film. Straight ahead at the base of the statue sat two bedraggled figures. One was Connie, and the other was Eugene. Both were filthy. Connie's unladylike posture was at odds with the long white dress she'd worn to dinner. Now stained and torn, the formal gown appeared even more romantic than when it was new, in a *Wuthering Heights*, lost-on-the-moors sort of way. Eugene, jacket clutched tight, sat slumped at Connie's side on the plinth.

Frankie struggled to get her own damp jacket back around her before her female form became as obvious to everybody here as Eugene's had been to Frankie.

She said, "Thank you again, Marietta. It doesn't seem real now, but I almost died back there."

"All part of a good day's work." Marietta loped across the gravel on her tough, bare, tomboy feet and slapped Luigi on the back.

"*Malatrice!*" Luigi growled.

Marietta said, "I told you, didn't I? By all that's holy, *I got the shot.*" She slashed her right arm in the air. "The flames traced a great arc over the sphinx's eye. As I predicted, the flame exactly bisected the pyramid's lit side and climbed up the obelisk like a golden monkey, to rest at the apex. I had to grab one of the studio cameras because you absconded — coward! So I filmed that perfect bit of footage myself."

Frankie stopped listening. She had more than film shots to think about. Now she knew for sure Connie was a treacherous friend, and she was fairly certain Eugene was a murderess.

Frankie approached the filthy pair.

She said coldly, "I see you got free, Connie. I'm happy, for your sake."

"I should hope so." Connie pulled her skirt straight. "But I must say I don't like your tone, Frankie."

"You almost got me and my tone killed," Frankie said. "However, I don't want to talk to you, Connie. I want to talk to your rescuer. Because I've been looking for her all day long."

"Who?" Connie asked.

"Me," Eugene answered. "She's been looking for me."

"Then she couldn't have been looking very hard." Connie glared at Frankie. "Any fool can find Eugene — the boy next door."

Several retorts occurred to Frankie, but she had no time for childish argument.

"I don't know your real name, *Eugene*," Frankie said. "But I do know that you've been lying to me from the start. You are not a man."

"How can you say that?" Connie protested. "Eugene bravely saved me from the fire. He was completely a man, and one to be admired and appreciated, so put that information in your stocking top."

Frankie gave Connie a withering glance. "You're not listening, Connie. *As* usual." She turned to Eugene. "You're not male — you are female. Dressed up, like me, to pass as a man."

"Eugene, you're a woman?" Connie demanded.

Eugene answered, "I'm tired, that's what I am."

Luigi rolled past with his camera and out of sight past the burned-out section of the set.

Frankie continued. "And that's not all, *Eugene*. You're *the* woman. You are the golden swimmer I saw with Gilbert Howard the night he died. The one he was kissing by the side of the pool."

Eugene buried her face in her hands.

Frankie asked, "How *could* you fall in love with a ladykiller like Gilbert Howard?"

"I'm not the first woman to cry over a man who betrayed her," Eugene said. "I'm not the first woman to mourn her own true love."

Connie stared. "Howie loved *you?* Of all the women in the world, he loved *you?*"

"Isn't it a funny old world?" Eugene said.

Frankie wondered how Eugene could joke at such a moment. "Gilbert Howard loved you, and you killed him."

In the pause that followed, Marietta's laugh rang out. Marietta ran lightly over the gravel toward them and threw herself down next to Eugene on the statue's base, bare feet splayed out in front of her. She said, "Frank, don't be an idiot. Eugene didn't kill Howie. She — Eugene — was with me last night."

"Will you swear to that, to the police?"

"Of course." Marietta squeezed Eugene's arm. "I'll swear in church if you need me to, Frank Achilles."

"In a court of law would do." Would a court of law believe Marietta? Probably.

But did Frankie believe her? She was not ready to say, either way. Frankie had a number of questions to ask Eugene, and no intention of accepting Marietta's unsupported word.

But before she could begin, Marietta did. "Well, Eugene, my old friend! Wipe your tears and celebrate the fact that we're all alive and I got the best shot in Samson's whole fire. And you, the red-headed hopeful," Marietta said to Connie. "What a night you're having! I'm only sorry Howie isn't here to see it."

Trust Marietta to send any conversation wheeling off Frankie's track and onto her own. An ethics question flashed through Frankie's mind: *How do you tell somebody who just saved your life to be silent, or preferably to go to Hades?*

She set the subject back on its course. "Eugene, can you prove you were with Marietta last night?"

Eugene stared down at the gravel between the knees of her men's trousers.

"Eugene was with me," Marietta insisted. "Will you get off that hobby horse, Frank Achilles? Yesterday you told my sister Billie that Leo Samson was guilty of killing Gilbert. Leo! A fellow who wouldn't slap a mosquito, let alone shoot a man. If you weren't so set on believing in women directors, I'd begin to doubt your judgment."

Since Marietta was doing all the talking, Frankie decided that the actress ought to at least do some of the answering as well. "Marietta, *can* you and Eugene prove you were together last night when Gilbert Howard was killed?"

"You're handsomer when you don't speak, Frank," Marietta said peevishly. Then, to Connie, she said "Well, you redhead, you're a pain in the whatsits, but you've got guts. How did you end up in the fire?"

Frankie glowered at this new change of subject. But honestly, she wanted to know the answer as well.

Connie leaned against one of the horse statue's legs and let out a long, tired-sounding sigh. "Ambition. Like the title of Samson's movie. Samson said he was going to use me in some of the shots in the fire, but he left a message with the doorman at Camillo's to say he'd cancelled my shot. The note didn't even explain *why* he'd cancelled. After all the build-up and publicity yesterday! Now I wonder whether he was ever really going to use me."

"Bless you for your innocent mind." Marietta smiled. "Sammy's not the first producer to try that nasty little trick with one of his actresses. I tried to explain it to you before, when we were having our lovely evening out at Camillo's Bar and Grille. Sammy was throwing his weight around, using you, the phony starlet, to bring me into line and stop trying to direct films. He tried to frighten me with you — the beautiful new face."

Frankie was determined to move the subject of murder back onto its course. But she couldn't resist saying to Connie, "I told you so. Like at the audition in Vancouver — King Samson was using you then, too."

"It makes me so mad I could kick that grumpy so-and-so producer." Connie peered from one side of the set to the other as if reliving a moment of decision. "But I thought that maybe I could sneak myself onto the film. If I made an entrance out of the flames and got myself into the shot anyway, a film editor might take the film and use it in *The Emperor of New York.* And then they'd have to use me in the film. Now the whole idea seems stupid."

Marietta said, "Yes, redhead. It was."

Connie isn't stupid. She's a complicated thinker. But Frankie didn't say it. She would not come to Connie's defence. Never again.

With a rustle of taffeta, Connie stood up. She walked around Eugene and Marietta and squashed down next to Frankie. Frankie pulled back, and Connie frowned. "You're acting horrible, Frankie."

Frankie gazed at Connie's stricken, dirty face and felt nothing of the old friendship. "Leave me alone, Connie. Why don't you go home to Vancouver?"

That ought to do it. Yes, even in the flickering light, Frankie knew the colour was rising in her old friend's cheeks. Those eyebrows of hers rose at a dangerous angle, one that Frankie knew too well.

Connie said, "I'm never going back to Vancouver. And I might never speak to you again. So, Frankie, this is your last chance. *What do you want in a friend?"*

Frankie knew what Connie expected of her: to make light of the situation. To say in radio announcer tones, *Friends are good to the la-a-ast drop.* Or, *If you want to get ahead, get a friend with a hat.* Or, *A friend gets you twice as much for a nickel.* Frankie had played her part since she and Connie were children. But Frankie had never felt less like a child than she did at that moment.

Frankie said, "What do I want in a friend? I would like somebody who is grown-up enough to apologize for all the bad things she has done to me in the course of the time we have known each other."

"Is that right? Well, tough luck." Connie rubbed at her face with blackened fists. The blotches stood out strongly against her pale face and white gown. Then she turned on her heel and walked away between the two sound stages that led to the extras' coffee yard and the gate to the outside world.

The last Frankie saw of Connie was her torn and dirty white dress vanishing around the corner that led out to Sunset Boulevard. She looked down at her men's brogues and traced half circles in the gravel, first left and then right. She tried to feel sorry to see Connie go. She tried to remember what it felt like to be her best friend, without question or reservation. She could not.

"My, my," Eugene said. "Not so clever and kind anymore, Frankie?"

Frankie said, "You knew about my disguise. So why didn't you tell me about *yours?*"

"I'm not an actress like you are, Frankie."

"You're a pretty darned good one," Frankie said bitterly. "What should I call you now that I know you're not 'Eugene'?"

Eugene frowned. "What does it matter? Everybody calls me Eugene now."

"What is your real name?" Frankie asked again, more fiercely.

"Elaine. But call me Eugene. I prefer it. Gilbert named me that way."

"Why would he call you by a man's name?"

"He thought women who acted like men were fun."

"I'm not surprised."

"And I travelled here from Eugene, Oregon. So that's what Gilbert called me."

"Like you call a fellow from Texas 'Tex'?" Frankie nodded. "All right, Eugene. Answer my question. How long have you been masquerading as male?" But Eugene had already told her the answer to her question when he'd talked about Bruno's career as a child actor. *There are problems with pretending to be somebody else for any length of time. Day after day, it eats the soul.*

"The Queen first dressed me as a man a year ago, so I could come and go unnoticed from Gilbert's place in the Garden of Allah."

"She dressed you, too?" Frankie shook her head.

"So that people wouldn't know about Gilbert and me. Wouldn't know that we were together forever, even though he couldn't marry me." Eugene blinked. "*Wouldn't* marry me. Dressed like this, I kept my privacy from the newspapers and he kept his reputation as a ladies' man."

Marietta added, "And his freedom to be a ladies' man."

Don't fall in love in Paradise Gardens. That warning was inspiration enough to any girl to fall, and fall hard, for the first fellow she saw.

A long pause hung like a cloud of smoke in the night air.

Even the Queen had deceived Frankie by not telling her straight out that Eugene was a woman. Eugene was right. Frankie didn't have a friend left in the world.

But Eugene did. She had Marietta. And, if she had Marietta for an ally, she also had the actress's sister, Billie Starr. The connection between these friends was obvious now — and should have been, since the first moment Frankie had found Marietta crying outside Eugene's villa. Now Marietta was providing Eugene with an alibi.

How could Frankie believe it? Or disprove it?

BAR HOPPING FOR ASTRONAUTS

Leo X Robertson

Leo X Robertson *is a Scottish process engineer, writer, and filmmaker, currently living in Stavanger, Norway. His first* Pulp Literature *appearance, 'Snapshots' (Issue 22), was reprinted in* Best of British Science Fiction 2019. *He has two novellas out this year:* The Grimhaven Disaster *(Unnerving, 2021) and* The Glow *with Aurelia Leo. He is currently working on a horror feature film that takes place entirely in the creepy basement of a local art studio. Find him on Twitter @Leoxwrite or check out his website* leoxrobertson.wordpress.com.

$\mathscr{B}$ar Hopping for Astronauts

Dodgy bars, like this one, sport fake women and real bartenders. The opposite of what a mostly male clientele wants. But the astronaut isn't picky anymore. Besides, he doesn't much mind the prospect of spending an evening in the company of robostrippers, their skins torn and peeling, the ragged mechanics of their limbs peering through. Decay into obsolescence merely adds to their humanity.

He finds a stool at the bar's far end and sits, leaning his rubber-sheathed elbows on the counter's stinking wood. Govcams on the walls turn to him, but amber rings of light around their lenses signify inactivity. 'Manually disabled', no doubt, by local glowlife gangs.

Flies buzz lazily between beer puddles. A blonde woman shoots him a sneering glance as she walks back to her posse of friends, all of them with glossy hair and clear heels. They gossip in tight circles, their thin voices needling in his ears. Through the chip in his head, he mentally pings a noise reduction to his helmet, reducing their sound by fifty percent.

The middle-aged bartender approaches, his metallic pupils glowing, bloodshot streaks firing out across his corneas.

Black market implants — for what purpose, the astronaut doesn't know.

The bartender doesn't react to the astronaut's suit or to the darkened smartglass visor covering his face. If people asked about that stuff here, the clientele would vanish. He says something, muffled words with a rising inflection.

The astronaut de-mutes.

"Drink," the bartender says, miming a glass.

"Do you do Lunar Juleps?" he asks.

"We might've lost it a few barware updates ago, but I'll check." He eventually returns with a dirty highball of slime-green fluid.

The astronaut dips his finger into the glass, and his glove sucks it all up. Nanites metabolize the alcohol for him before the drink even reaches his bloodstream. Nanites are many things, but fun isn't one of them.

As the astronaut tries to place the highball back on the bar without causing a fuss, he feels people looking at him funny. The gecko pad of his palm sticks to the glass like Velcro. He carefully unpeels it.

The bartender sighs. "What the hell are you doing here?"

"Huh?"

"By the looks of your suit, you must be, what, late sixties? Try the Caloris District. You know Tycho Singles? That's more your speed."

The astronaut shakes his head. "They don't let me in with the helmet on."

"Then take it off."

"I can't!"

"I'm not babysitting some dementia-ridden old coot, okay? I'll do you this one last courtesy. Then be on your way." The bartender eyes up the suit. "I can see the flap for the emergency cord from here. The red one, right? Here, I'll get it——"

The astronaut bats the hand away. He turns and pushes through the throng, heading back outside.

He catches his breath in the street. Snow stills the air, quelling the city noise. Teens pass him by, shooing pesky ad drones that quiz them about alcohol consumption and sexual appetites. Strumpbots stand at regular intervals, maximally optimizing the sidewalk's revenue without intruding upon one another's territory.

White clouds of vape juice bloom before him, and the nanites, alerted to this anomaly, replicate the smell for him in his helmet. Cotton candy, mingling with poor-quality weed.

Red light shimmers off the astronaut's visor. It settles on his chest as a flickering laser dot. He traces its source to the thick black bangle of a glowlife with a blonde quiff, who leans on a nearby defunct autocab.

"Pew pew!" the glowlife says, making finger guns.

The astronaut flinches.

A woman in the glowlife crew laughs. She has studs of metal pierced seemingly at random across her face. Braids of light in her hair stream rainbow colours. Dog holos caper around her poodle skirt. "He actually thought you were firing at him! Old man, you think that's possible?"

"What's his suit all about?" says the third guy in the posse. A green animated graffiti tag shimmers on his muscle tee, and red biotats of demons smirk on his deltoids.

Quiff cocks his head. "Is that the Vitus New Moon model?"

"What's Vitus?" Poodle Skirt says. "Oh, wait." She sings the Vitus jingle: *"Overcoming limits of biology / Colonising space with technology!"*

"Weren't those ads from, like, the seventies?" Biotats says.

"Dude, how old are you?" Quiff says.

The astronaut can't help himself. The words bubble up inside him. "I-I was on the moon."

"Hah!" Quiff says. "Who wasn't? I was there last week."

"I got back yesterday," Biotats says.

Poodle Skirt spits. "You can take the suit off now."

The astronaut walks away, but Quiff grabs his shoulder, takes out a blade and slices the suit open.

In a reflex, the astronaut slaps his hand over the opening.

"Sorry," Quiff says, "did I breach your suit?"

The friends rush over and tug at the rip, tearing the suit all over. The astronaut wrestles them off and runs away, their mocking laughter trailing behind him.

Sleek-looking autocabs roll up beside him and open their doors. "Sir," they say, "you look tired. May I assist?"

He doesn't live far away enough to risk falling victim to a hacked cab's kidnapping protocol — or worse, so he walks all the way home in the snow.

He arrives home with the suit almost completely peeled off, revealing the T-shirt and long underwear he has on beneath. The suit doesn't know what to do, and self-repair only causes further damage. After all, if this were space, the astronaut would be dead by now. Its warning sirens blare inside the helmet, ringing madly in his ears.

He screams, clawing at the suit. Nanites in the material melt its torn edges, reaching out at each other in silvery threads, trying to knit the seams back together. But the tears are too big, the nanites too far from one another. As programmed, they try to stick the suit to his skin. In ultra-critical conditions, better to create any kind of seal and let a patch of skin get frostbite or sunburn than to do nothing and risk a fatality. That's the theory in space. Here on Earth, melted polymer scalds his chest. He tugs the suit off and leaves it in scraps on the floor.

He walks through to his living room, tearing away the T-shirt and picking strips of burnt rubber off his naked torso.

"Sir! Were you assaulted?" Jenny's voice comes from the ceiling's speaker. "We ought to file a report—"

The astronaut waves his hand. "Don't fuss."

"It's no fuss, sir," she says. "I'm not real."

"I know, Jenny. You don't have to remind me."

He sits on the edge of his couch, balancing the helmet so it doesn't fall. Empty foodule packets litter the table in front of him, and dirty bootprints coat the carpet.

As his adrenaline subsides, the apartment's chill rushes over him. He hadn't noticed how comfy the suit was, how like a second skin. Its sensations had become sensory background noise. Now, he's palpably bare.

Out the window, a haze of neon blends the buildings together, a dim redness on the horizon revealing the outline of so many concrete blocks all seemingly fused into one.

One last scrap of the suit flops off his shoulder. He examines it with a sorry glance. Nanite threads glint silver. In space, they bridged together throughout the suit to keep it firm during pressurization. They agglomerated where needed across the suit's many membranes. Made repairs. Relayed biomedical data. Vaporized micrometeoroids. Expelled carbon dioxide and water vapour. They strung together into synthetic veins, sending cooling water coursing across his skin. They eradicated dead cells and other detritus from his surface, and other excreta from elsewhere.

He goes to the window and opens the delivery box. Shiny foodule packets spill to the floor. Out of habit, he picks one up and squeezes it. That was usually all it took for nanites to suck out the juices and inject nutrients into him like reverse mosquitoes. Not anymore.

He closes the box and orders some pyjamas on its touchscreen.

"Connect me to Vitus support team, please?" he asks his visor.

Ellipses flash inside the visor as it makes the call for him.

A smiling cartoon face appears. "Hi!" says a female voice. "Did you mean to reach me? I heard something about Vitus."

"Yeah, I need repair for a New Moon."

"Sorry, sir, we no longer offer support for that model. May I order you a replacement?"

"I can't afford that. I couldn't even afford my Vitus. They gave it to me after I——"

"Would you like to hear more about our latest, the Tharsis? It's a flexible and durable polymer suit with——"

"I want to go back inside! Now!"

"Sir, yelling isn't good for your health. Just saying. I don't mind it, of course. I'm not real."

He pulls the helmet off and throws it to the floor. Instead of smashing, it dents the wooden boards with a *dunk*.

"Sir?" the AI says.

He leans on the wall, sliding down, hugging his knees. The suit kept his skin young, supple, hairless.

"Intruder! Intruder!" Jenny says.

He looks to the ceiling. "Settle down, Jenny. It's still me."

"Voice recognition confirmed, sir. Glad to see you again. You look different! New haircut?"

He feels the perfectly trimmed bald pate. It seems to itch only now the nanites have gone. "Good different?" he says.

"Why not see for yourself?"

He grits his teeth, then gets up and heads to the bathroom.

"By the way," Jenny says from her speaker in the tiled wall, "you forgot your pills again, silly billy."

The mirror spits a handful of green liquid capsules onto a ceramic dish.

"Thanks, Jenny." He picks one up and squeezes it with thumb and forefinger, again to no avail. He sighs, winces, and looks at his face.

He'd seen warped glimpses on the visor's inner surface, or reflected dimly in puddles and shop windows sometimes, but always softened by the smartglass's resting darkness setting. The unmasked thing is something else. Sunken eyes. Thin lips. Incipient jowls. Wrinkles like deep gouges sliced across his forehead.

"Handsome as ever, sir," Jenny says.

"Well, Jenny," he says, "that's the visor off. All my settings are disabled. You might as well tell me the year now. I can't block it out."

"You sure?"

"Yep."

She tells him.

His mouth gapes, revealing pale, receding gums. "I've been in that suit for twenty-two years?"

"Yup."

He shrugs. "Time flies when you barely leave the house."

"Would you like to know anything else? How about the latest water shortage on Mars? Want to know what happened with that organ cloning scandal? There's talk of a new viral epidemic in a biohab——"

"That's enough crisis for one day, thanks. I'm going to bed."

Light wakes him up. It's Jenny, warming him with an artificial sun from the screen in his bedroom ceiling.

He groans. "Disengage protocol, Jenny!"

"I may only have seen your new face for fourteen hours and twenty-six minutes," Jenny says, "but to my vast knowledge base, most humans don't display an expression *that* consistently sad. Especially not in their sleep. So come on, get up."

He slams a pillow over his face.

"Sir?" Jenny says. "I was thinking. I'm not real, but I do think."

The pillow muffles his words. "Again, Jenny, I know how this works."

"Great! Look, you know I would never wish you any harm. I'm literally incapable of doing so. But maybe what happened to you wasn't the worst."

"I don't want to hear this right now."

"But it might do you some good, and that's what I'm here for!"

He stays quiet.

"I thought of something that might cheer you up. Go look in your delivery box!"

He lies there, immobile. Jenny ramps up the light intensity until it makes an unhealthy whining sound.

"Fine!" He gets up, tosses the pillow aside and heads to the living room.

In the box are the clothes he ordered yesterday and a clear

vacuum bag with a pre-sliced pizza inside, squished until its orange oils run into the plastic's creases.

He reaches for the T-shirt and joggers but withdraws his hand like he just touched an iron. The screen on the box reads 60°C.

"To keep the pizza toasty!" Jenny says. "And I had it ordered in that bag so your clothes wouldn't smell."

"Very considerate of you, Jenny."

He unzips the bag, its plastic relaxing, and slides the pizza onto the table. Its smell is familiar and distant.

He tugs at the crust, dislodges a slice and—

"Ow!"

"Sir?"

"I forgot how to use my tongue."

"Well—take care."

"Okay, okay!"

He tries again. Mozzarella melts over his taste buds, accompanied by a tang of tomato sauce. He bites down on a crunchy piece of pepperoni, burnt a little on the edges, but it hardly matters. "Mm!"

"What do you think?"

"This is amazing," he says between chews.

"I'm glad!"

A piece falls out of his mouth. He smiles up at the ceiling. "I need more eating practice, though. What will we try next?"

"Oh, I'm so happy this worked, sir! We'll try whatever you want!"

He frowns. "Wait, wait."

"What is it?"

He grimaces. "Can you show me a video of someone putting on clothes? Project it onto one of the walls once you've got it."

"Uh, sir, did you mean 'taking off clothes'? I know this is the first time you've requested such a thing, but as always, I'm not a real person. Couldn't judge you if I wanted to."

"Ugh." He looks up at the ceiling as he goes back to the box, lifting the clothes out and brandishing them accusingly at Jenny. He shuffles out the long underwear, puts the T-shirt on backwards, and nearly falls over when slipping on the joggers. He crosses his legs on the floor and catches his breath.

"Sir, was that necessary? Please be strong enough to clarify your requests for help in future."

"Yes, Jenny."

"Back to it, then?"

"Yeah. Hey, get me a coffee!"

It's not long before a drone buzzes by, dropping an insulated pouch into the box.

He opens the door from the inside and takes the pouch to the kitchen, where he pours its contents into the one clean glass he uses to top up his hydration. Out of habit, he dips his finger into the brown liquid.

"Ouch!"

His skin is tender, like it's missing a few layers. More than a few.

He takes a sip. "Delicious."

"Cool! What now?"

"Surprise me."

Over the next few hours, Jenny delivers an assortment of test objects.

He thumbs books and savours the crisp feel of their freshly printed paper. He spritzes himself in the face with a cologne bottle, catching himself in the eyes, but the scent of citrus and sandalwood seems worth it. He even sticks his finger in a little plastic prank toy that gives him an electric shock.

"Play me some music," he asks Jenny.

"What kind?"

"Anything, anything!"

Noise blares into the room. It sounds like static from an old radio that's clattering around in a washing machine.

"What the hell, Jenny? I said 'music'."

"It's from a local stream," she says like a partner taking offence on behalf of her choice.

"No, no, give me — jazz. Play me some jazz."

The reedy sound of a saxophone fills his ears, and notes from a double bass reverberate around the living room. The soft hiss of drum brushes makes his skin shiver. He grips his head, closes his eyes, and grins. His eyes flicker open, and he bolts to the window, unlocking the latch and pushing back the glass.

"Sir, no!"

"Relax." He sticks his head out.

Drones buzz by like big cicadas. A nearby advert simulates the sound of a rushing waterfall. Several stories below, autocabs shout robotic warnings at pedestrians.

The breeze rushes over his face. It's thick as a blanket and pungent with smog, but he doesn't care.

"What is it, sir?" Jenny asks.

He's crying now. "It's wonderful."

Sensory exploration soon begets the difficult work of relearning old habits. The nanites have gone, so they can't baby him anymore. He has to shower, brush his teeth, clip his nails, and shave without nicking himself.

Days and weeks pass in frustration. Soon, he's back in bed again, refusing to get up.

Jenny beams her light over him. "Sir, it's time to wash the sheets. It's been over a month since suitgate. You're entraining dirt everywhere."

He's silent.

"I had another idea, if you wanna hear it."

"You're just gonna tell me anyway."

"Remember Tycho Singles?"

He pushes the sheets back like an insolent teen. "What about it?"

"Why not go back there? It still has a consistent four-point-two rating, above average for the area. You used to love it back when——"

"I was young, happy, famous, successful, and rich. Cheers, Jenny."

"Oh, please."

He shuts his eyes in thought and pinches the bridge of his nose. "I've passed by there before. It used to be young and happening. Looks like the same crowd has hung around there for decades. So now it's——"

"Still an age-appropriate place for a gent like yourself?"

He kicks the covers off and looks at the ceiling. "You getting cheeky with me?"

"Did I violate a boundary? Are you dissatisfied with your service? Because I can always——"

"It's fine. I like it."

"Good. Because I took just *one* more additional liberty."

"Did you, now?"

"Go take a look in the box!" Her autotuned squeal grates in his ears.

"Fine!" He gets up and heads to the living room.

In the box is a full tuxedo and black bowtie.

"Jenny, can you tell me your budget settings again?"

"Of course, but why?"

"You think I can afford fancy clothes and expensive cocktails?"

"Not all the time." Jenny adopts the tone of a benevolently scheming wife trying to sound nonchalant. "But you deserve to celebrate your progress."

Tuxed up, he hesitates as he approaches the facial recognition scanner at Tycho Singles—but it gives him the green light and invites him in. He reaches up to feel the helmet, but it's long gone now.

Tycho is much nicer than the last bar he chose for himself. Ornate cornices, white pillars, bronze light fixtures.

As he walks in, his new dress shoes clacking pleasantly on the lacquered hardwood floor, he notices how much lower-tech the bar is than the average locale. There's a champagne fountain holo here, an android waiter there, but not much. Surely because of the clientele. All around, sophisticated elders on dates sit around tables of expensive marble.

Why would he want to hang out with all these old people?

Oh. Right. He's one of them.

He approaches the bar and sits down. A woman nearby catches his eye. She has delicate wrinkles under her eyes and her hair is in a high, silvery do. Placid waves roll over the fabscreen of her dress.

He stares at the marble counter, too nervous to make an introduction.

"What'll it be, sir?" A bot-tender in a white tux wheels himself over. Its head is a gunmetal cylinder, and a screen on the front shows its few emotions in Technicolor pixels. "A quiet type, eh? I can offer you a recommendation."

He nods.

A green circle loads to completion on its face. "For an esteemed gent like yourself? A Lunar Julep." A door opens on its chest and a silver cup appears. A small tap deposits the julep inside, and the bot-tender places it on the table.

The cup gathers frost. He reaches out to touch it, startled by how cold it feels. He peers at the green liquid within and brings his index finger to its surface before remembering. He stops and, as practised, raises the drink to his lips with both hands, taking a sip.

He coughs.

"Sir? You don't like it?"

"It's fine. It's just—got a kick." Alcohol rushes straight to his brain. "Whew!"

"I recognize that voice, sir," the bot-tender says. "Have you been here before?"

He lowers his head. "A long time ago."

"I thought so. I'm examining some photos of us from the seventies." Its blocky eyebrows pinch in a frown. "Huh. You sure looked different. You're wearing something weird. Do you remember? There are all these women crowded around you. You were sitting about where you are now. But you had much more company back then."

"I don't really wanna talk about it."

The bot-tender leans in. "Well, I can't just leave you here."

"Yes, you can."

"It makes the other patrons awkward. If you want to sit here, we have to talk about *something*."

They're both silent.

"Hey," the bot-tender says, "you were in pay grade XZ back then. Impressive!"

"I can take it from here." The wave-dressed woman has a sultry, gravelly voice. "What brings you to Tycho?"

He dares to meet her eyes briefly, then looks back at the counter. "I'm, uh, supposed to be celebrating."

"Cheers to you, then." She raises her martini. "May I ask the occasion, Mr … ?"

The words form in his throat. The stream of all he's ever been before. He stifles it, his face contorting with worry.

"Sir!"

He turns.

It's the scanner on the door, addressing someone outside. "I can't let you in if you insist on covering your face."

On the street is a man in a grass-green Vitus New Moon. The helmet's visor is dark, his shoulders slumped.

"Friend of yours?" the woman says.

He smiles at her. "Just might be. Excuse me for a moment?"

She nods, and he walks back to the door.

"I used to come here all the time!" says the astronaut in the green suit.

"We both did," he says.

The visor swivels, fishbowling all it reflects.

Who's that old guy in the tux? Oh, it's me.

"I don't know you," the astronaut says.

"Yes, you do. You just don't recognize me." As he approaches, the chip in his head illuminates the surname *Zhang* on the suit.

Zhang looks down at his chest. His shoulders square and relax. "I haven't seen it do that in a long time. Who are you?"

"Bob Jones?" Bob says. It sounds painfully ordinary out loud, but it's his name nonetheless.

The astronaut takes some tint out of the smartglass visor. The tired face of an elderly Asian gent appears, his hair thinning and silvery with nanites. "It *is* you! What were you, an engineer?"

Bob nods.

The astronaut taps his chest. "Mike Zhang. I was an architect, see? Green suit!"

"I remember."

"Am I glad I ran into you! No one else gets it anymore. The importance of what we did, that is." He bumps Bob on the arm with a fist. "These days there are colonies all over, but *we* made the moon habitable, man. We were pioneers!" Mike looks at the bar. "They used to let me in here dressed like this when we came back. You remember?"

Bob nods.

Mike pats his chest. "People went to bed with me while I was in this suit." He smiles. "Felt like it would be that way forever."

Bob puts his hand on Mike's shoulder. "Now it's almost like it never happened." The suit warms his hand as nanites cross its external membrane to assess the threat.

"But w-we're trailblazers," Mike says. "We got to do more than most ever could."

"At the time." Bob smiles sympathetically.

Mike mirrors the smile. "Yeah." A thought makes him shudder with excitement. "What are you doing now? Let's go talk about the mission! Hey, remember that time we thought we'd lost two whole oxygen bottle racks? Or when Montero welded himself to an airlock and we thought he'd die if we tried to remove him?" He made fists of his hands. "What do you say? Wanna go grab a drink somewhere else?"

Bob bites his lip. He looks at Mike, then back to the bar, where the wave-dressed woman raises her glass to him.

"If it's okay with you," Bob says, "I think I'll go back inside."

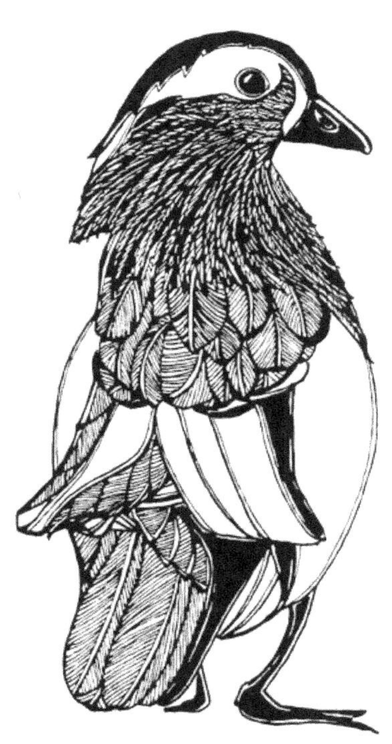

BHUT

Michelle F Goddard

Michelle F Goddard *is a vocalist and musician who has performed around the world, and a composer with credits for work in musicals and films. Her short fiction has been published in B Cubed Press's* Alternative Apocalypse *anthology, Ulthar Press's* Machinations and Mesmerism *anthology, and* Hybrid Fiction *magazine, among others. She is presently working on several short stories and a science fiction novel. You can find her at michellefgoddard.wordpress.com.*

$\mathcal{B}$HUT

Claudia found her husband leaning over her pot of spaghetti, spoon in one hand and a jar of cayenne in the other.

"You know I can see you, right?" she said, as she marched toward him. She took the jar and shouldered him away from the stove.

"It just needs a little more heat," Rudy said, handing her the spoon.

"I'll tell you what needs a little more heat," she said, eyeing her husband up and down. She threw out the enticement, but it landed like a plane on a thirty-minute layover: no one was getting off.

Rudy retreated to the breakfast table and pulled up the headlines on his laptop. "Your sauce would be amazing if you added a bit more kick. "Do you see this? Some guy comes up with a new kind of granola, and he's making millions. He's got a life-sized cut-out displayed at the grocery store. I mean, everyone knows who he is."

"I also hear he and his wife are divorcing and fighting over his actual net worth," Claudia said. "There's always a price for fame."

Rudy dismissed her with a wave. "Not us, babe. We jar that sauce, slap my handsome mug on the label, and we're laughing. That is, once you add a few more Scovilles."

Claudia covered the pot and dropped the spoon in the sink. She stepped toward her husband. Rudy reached out and encircled her waist without looking. His other hand scrolled through the news. She twisted her fingers through his curls. The touches of grey and the few extra pounds did nothing to quell her desire for him. Lately, however, Rudy seemed distracted. The only things that got him fired up were the hot peppers he ate morning, noon, and night.

Claudia pressed herself against him, even to the point of thrusting her ample breast against his cheek. Rudy did not release his grip on her, but he did move his face slightly so that he could continue reading. Claudia sighed. Maybe she should be happy his midlife crisis hadn't gone the way of alcoholism or fast cars.

"And why not my mug on the jar of spaghetti sauce?" Claudia asked.

"Oh, babe. You wouldn't be able to stand the heat." Rudy slapped her on the ass before sliding his arm out to reach toward a bowl set out on the middle of the table. In it stood a collection of peppers, washed and dried. Rudy plucked one fat, green jalapeño by its stem. He took a bite and chewed vigorously as he continued to read. "But I'm telling you, you've got to tweak that recipe."

Claudia stepped away and untied the apron from around her neck. "Well, if you're so keen to give me advice, maybe you should come with me to the farmers' market."

"But I'm reading."

"All those reality stars and overnight successes will be waiting for you when you come back. Maybe you could spend some time with me." She put her hands on her hips when he didn't move. "You're the one nagging me about ingredients."

Rudy rolled his eyes, but he did exit the webpage and close the lid on his laptop.

Claudia held his hand, not minding in the least that she almost had to pull him across the parking lot. However, once they had walked through a garlanded bower, the provisional entrance to the market, Rudy picked up the pace. He headed to a large sign that displayed cartoon pigs happily marinating themselves and chickens gleefully roosting in roasting pans. The top of the sign was decorated with flying pies, and the caption read, *Soar to New Heights. Enter the Food Fair Competitions.*

"You see?" Rudy said. "This is what I'm telling you." He grabbed a form from the doe-eyed young woman dressed in a straw hat, gingham, and short shorts. "Everyone cheering as we accept the blue ribbon. Buyers clamouring to get our sauce on the shelves. Fame and fortune, baby. Fame. And. Fortune." He held out the paper, practically pushing it into Claudia's chest. She took it and stuffed it into her purse, glancing around as Rudy's unbound enthusiasm drew eyes to him. "But that sauce of yours has got to stand out. You know how many people think they're the new Ragu? The internet is littered with wannabes. We need an edge. An angle."

"You mean a gimmick? Can't it just be really good sauce? The kind you put over pasta?"

"Are you nuts? It's got to be something people can't figure out, like a mystery ingredient, something impossible to copy."

"Why don't we say there's pixie dust in it?"

"Would you get serious, please? It's bad enough you don't take my suggestion to add some more chilies to the stuff we eat at home, but now we're talking business. We're talking about the public. They want something different. Something amazing."

"You want something amazing," a voice said, "you should try my peppers."

They turned to find a man smiling at them. He held out his hand. "Stanley Wong."

Claudia shook his hand but stared at him askance. "And how are your peppers amazing?"

"Well, I grow them myself, and I come from a long line of Szechuan farmers. You are familiar with that spicy cuisine? I have mastered mystical arts to entice the most robust properties of these delectable gifts from the genus capsicum."

"See?" Rudy said, nudging her with his elbow. "This guy knows about marketing."

"Capsicum is a genus of flowering plants in the nightshade family, Solanaceæ," Stanley said. "Not to be confused with capsaicin which is the chemical compound that makes chili peppers hot."

"Are you really from Sichuan province?" Claudia asked.

"Who cares?" Rudy said, eyeing the wide assortment of row upon row of red, green, orange, and yellow peppers. "So, whaddaya got there?

"Some rare and truly lively varieties," Stanley said.

"And hot? I don't see the point of a pepper unless it's hot."

"My friend, the hottest. I should really put a warning on some of these."

"I'll be the judge of that," Rudy said, staring at the two-inch flame on a stem. "But they don't look that exotic. That one there just looks like a regular chili."

"Ah, the Tien Tsin chili. Native to the Tien Tsin province of China, it can reach up to 75,000 Scovilles, making it very hot. In Chinese, they're described as 'chao tian jiao' or 'reaching skyward'. It is a staple of Sichuan and Hunan cuisine and a key ingredient in kung pao chicken."

"Can I try one?"

"It's really not an eating pepper. You wouldn't serve this with spinach dip."

Rudy held out his hand. "Understood."

"At least don't handle it bare-handed. Here," Stanley said, handing him the pepper speared on a plastic fork. "And don't say I didn't warn you."

Rudy popped the whole pepper in his mouth, spat the stem out into a nearby garbage, and chewed. "Not bad. Its flavour reminds me of Italian red peppers—a sort of pungent, musty taste."

Stanley folded his arms across his chest and stared at Rudy as if he were a math problem. After a moment, he smiled and nodded. "Have you ever heard of competitive eating?"

Claudia didn't have to drag Rudy out to the next farmers' market. He had to drag her. They wound past cheery tables stacked with homemade jams and organic honey. They meandered along fruit and vegetable stands spread across the aisles like brazen, Rubenesque women. Early corn roasted in its husks on smoking grills. Children screamed and waved as they rode ponies around a circular pen, and, in the distance, Claudia saw a stage and a band setting up.

"I don't like this," Claudia said.

"I know," Rudy said, scowling at the fiddler. "Country bands."

"Not that," Claudia said, swatting her husband.

"Stanley said he could get me in," Rudy said, "even though it's last minute. All I have to do is loiter around his pepper stand after I win."

"If you win."

"Oh. Nice. Thanks for the vote of confidence."

"You don't need any help from me. There's only one person on that ballot. And he's crazy."

"Hey. Come on, now."

"No. Do you know what this could do to you? There was a guy who burned a one-inch hole in his œsophagus."

"Just from eating a pepper?"

"Well, no. Not *a* pepper. Many. And the injury was from the throwing up he did after he ate them."

"Then I guess I'd better not throw up. Hear that, asshole? It's all on you."

"Don't joke."

"My butt doesn't think this is funny at all. But it's ready to take one for the team. It's one-hundred-percent behind me."

"Okay. Fine. Be that way."

An hour later, two women and four men, Rudy included, walked onto the stage. Each competitor took a seat at a long table. In front of each there was a clear glass bowl full of gnarly-looking red Jamaican hot chili peppers. Beside that stood a tall glass of milk and a smaller, empty bowl.

"Welcome, one and all," Mr Fitzwiggin, the fair manager and competition host, said into the microphone. "This competition is not for the faint of heart, but for those who got the stomach to eat and those who got the stomach to watch, we're gonna get this going in just five minutes. Give everyone a chance to high-tail it over here. You do not want to miss this. And while we're waiting, just want to throw out a thank-you to Mr Wong, our neighbourhood pepper aficionado. He's the one who's supplied the culinary sacrifices to our gods of amusement. Made sure they're good and hot, too."

Applause trickled from the crowd as Stanley took a moment to step onto the stage and wave. "Wong's Pepper Emporium," Stanley said, in a loud voice. "Come and visit."

"Now, the rules are," Mr Fitzwiggin said, glancing toward the contestants, "you got sixty seconds to get as many of these fat and juicy beauties down your gullet as you can. Any sign of spitting, and you're disqualified, so eat 'em clean and swallow it all down. Each of these has been weighed, and caps are assured, so you all make sure you put the stems in your counting bowls. No stem, and it just don't count. Got it?"

Nods from the participants was all the response he got. Everyone, including Rudy, stared at the bowl in front of them like it was Everest and they had a full tank of oxygen on their back and heating pads down their shorts.

Mr Fitzwiggin glanced out at the thickening crowd as he pulled out his stopwatch. "Ready, set, go!"

Hands reached for bowls. Peppers were plucked by the stems and red twisted nubs placed between teeth. Stems were pulled free and dropped into bowls as contestants jawed through the flesh of the peppers. The action repeated over and over. Throats swallowed, shoulders heaved, and eyes watered as the competitors dug their way through the bowls of tam-shaped bombs.

It was the longest sixty seconds Claudia had ever experienced. When it was over and Rudy stepped back, away from the almost empty bowl of peppers, Claudia felt her knees go weak. The other contestants drained their glasses of milk, the white liquid coursing down their cheeks as they gulped. Rudy drained his drink in one long, slow drought and then wiped his mouth with the back of his hand, obviously playing to the loud cheers of the crowd. He raised his hands in victory, the win apparent to anyone with eyes, as the losers staggered from the stage.

Relief filled Claudia's veins in a cool stream that had her shivering even as Rudy swung her off her feet.

"Did you see that?" Rudy said. "They loved me."

"I was right here," Claudia said, once she was back on terra firma. "I saw you."

"I ate twice as many as all of them combined. I kicked their butts."

"And your butt will kick you later."

"I feel great. Honestly. Left a nice little hum in my mouth. I could go again."

"Don't you dare."

"Stanley," Rudy said to the pepper vendor as he approached, "explain things to her."

"Actually, she's right. You need to do an interview," Stanley said, pointing to his pepper stand. "Over there."

"Oh, yeah," Rudy said, running a hand through his hair. "Ready for my close-up."

"It's radio."

"Whatever," Rudy said, undaunted.

For the rest of the spring and summer, every week was another fair or festival and another competition. At first, Claudia travelled with Rudy and visited little towns she didn't even know existed. Sometimes it was hours of travel time, all for sixty seconds on a stage and a bowl or plate of one pepper or another: jalapeño, habanero, or Scotch bonnet. A few competitions were sponsored by specialty stores, and Rudy downed pepper sauce, dark chocolate Tabasco squares, and something called Blazing Balls, a candy made with hot chili powder. He was even invited to judge a *Pants on Fire Chili Cook-Off.* He had begrudgingly indicated his winner with the caveat that it could be hotter. The other judges glared at him through watery eyes and overrunning noses.

Claudia was not able to accompany him to every fair, but Rudy didn't seem to mind. Crowds grew, and video of Rudy's wins popped up all over the internet. Wong's Pepper Emporium devoted a webpage to them while advertising its pepper-infused vinegars and oils. *Even if you can't eat them yourself, you can get a splash of the experience.* Reporters called for interviews. Even commuters hustling through the turnstile at Rudy's train station recognized him and stopped to chat. It helped that he had stuck up an article about himself in the window of the collector booth.

"You know," Rudy said after returning from another successful competition, "Stanley says if I really want to make it big, I should go for the Guinness Book of World Records."

"No," Claudia said, following him to the bathroom. Rudy closed the door, but she remained standing there with her hands on her hips. "No way," she yelled to the closed door. "That is not a good idea."

"Why not?" Rudy said, from inside the bathroom.

"Because you're pushing it as it is. All these competitions. They can't be good for you."

"I'm fine."

"Until you're not."

"Can we talk about this later?"

"You're the one who brought it up," Claudia said.

"But it's very distracting, Claudia."

"Oh, no. You did this on purpose. You can't just tell me about this and then tell me we can't talk about it. It's not fair, Rudy."

"Oh my god, my hand went through the TP."

"Oh. Oh, that's gross. I hate it when that happens. You catch the perforation and it's just, ugh … gross. Oh well, I guess I gotta get three-ply."

"No. Not like that." Rudy's voice shook. "I mean *through* through. All the way through. Like, I couldn't hold it. In my hand. The TP, not my poop. Though maybe I couldn't hold that either. Holy hell."

"Did your hand cramp? Did you miss the roll? Do you want me to come in there?"

"Hell, no. Just give me a minute."

Claudia heard heavy breathing from the other side of the door. She pressed her ear to the door. "Are you okay?"

"I think so." Water splashed into the sink. The doorknob turned, and Claudia stepped back as the door opened. Rudy stood there, looking faint. "That was weird."

"What happened?"

"I don't know. I think I'm just tired."

Claudia leaned back and peered at him, turning her head to see him in a different light, though the only light available was from the dim hallway light fixture. "You look strange. Pale. Like a ghost. I think you should lie down. Or maybe we should go to the hospital."

"The hospital?"

"Do I need to go over this with you again? Mouth ulcers. Heartburn, reflux, nausea. Stomach ulcers. Even asthma and seizures. Burning diarrhœa."

Rudy looked behind him. "All good there." He thumbed toward the bathroom. "Smell for yourself."

"You're being gross. There was an article about someone who

died eating peppers, you know."

"Yeah. He got Naga-ed to death. Get it? Because some peppers are called Naga. Get it?"

"You are hilarious. And I'm being serious. You might be fine now, but what about in the long run? You can't possibly do this forever."

Rudy shrugged as he walked toward the kitchen.

"And this is all well and good," Claudia said, trying another angle, "but you realize the only one making money is Stanley. You're up there eating peppers, and he's the one benefiting. We should start thinking about how we can make use of this for our future."

"Fine," Rudy said, choosing a pepper from the bowl. "What's your idea?"

Claudia watched him chew for a moment but chose to say nothing about the pepper. "We should sell my spaghetti sauce. Stanley said he would help me draw up a business plan and get a website up. He's already introduced us to lots of people at the farmers' markets, so we've got an in there. He's an invaluable resource. And he's willing to help us."

"Us?" Rudy said. "You seem to have lots of time to chat with Stanley when you should be watching me."

"Rudy!"

"Okay, okay. But while you work on that, I'm going to keep being me." He ate another pepper. "Besides, how much easier will it be to market your sauce if you've already got a recognizable name behind it?" He waved his hands out in front of him. "Burning Diarrhœa Sauce. It's the shit."

Claudia put a hand on his arm as he reached for another pepper. "I'm worried. What if I told you I want you to stop?"

Rudy shrugged. "I can stop whenever I want to."

"Can you?"

"Sure," Rudy said, the word sliding around the pepper in his mouth. "I just don't want to. It's not like this is heroin, you know."

The crowd surged. Calls for autographs and photos filled the air. Rudy turned to grin at everyone and everywhere, all at the same time. There was no room for Claudia in the milieu, and after being roundly jostled, she retreated, gasping, from the press of the mob. She found herself alone, her back pressed up against a table laid out with carrots, purple onions, and cabbage, the late summer vegetables' robust colours heralding the oncoming fall. Rudy looked around and, catching her eye, waved madly as if he were a kid on a rollercoaster ride.

"He really is something, isn't he?" Stanley said.

Claudia jumped at his sudden presence but then smiled. "Everyone knows him. He's very popular. I'm sure you can appreciate that. Don't your peppers get more attention when he's around?"

"They do. But I wonder. What about you? He seems awfully busy with his public. How much time is he spending with you?"

"We're fine, Stanley. In fact, we were just talking about our future. Maybe setting up a little stand for my spaghetti sauce."

"I'm glad you two are thinking about that. You're a beautiful, talented lady. I'd hate to see Rudy make you feel anything less than that. I certainly wouldn't want to risk losing someone like you if you were in my life."

Claudia blushed, suddenly aware of Stanley's deep brown eyes staring into hers, the smell of his cologne, how he had taken her hand in his, so smoothly, so gently that she had hardly realized it until now.

"Are these delicate hands ready for that kind of work?" Stanley said. He rubbed the palm of her hand with his thumb. "Maybe this is something we could do together. Your recipe, my ingredients and connections. We'd make an unstoppable team."

"Hey. What's wrong with your hand?" Rudy asked, as he broke free from the throng. He pulled Claudia's hand from Stanley's. "Did you get hurt by my adoring fans?"

Claudia slid her hand from Rudy's and folded her arms. "I'm fine. We were just discussing my spaghetti sauce."

"*Our* spaghetti sauce. I mean, whose cardboard cut-out is going to be standing next to the display, right?" He put his arm around Claudia and drew her close.

"Stanley was saying it'll be a lot of work. You'll have to commit."

"I'll commit. I'm committed." He looked back and forth between their faces, his own growing sterner.

"When?"

"Look, bub. Nothing gets done in this world anymore without marketing. You could have the dumbest, most useless idea, but if you can convince enough people that it isn't, you're golden."

Claudia turned to stare at her husband. "Are you saying the sauce isn't any good?"

"No, and stop putting words in my mouth. I'm saying that what I'm doing is creating brand recognition." Rudy glared at Stanley. "You should know. What were you before I came along? Some guy with a bunch of peppers no one even knew about? I put you on the map. I'll do the same for the spaghetti sauce. Just you watch."

"How?" Stanley said.

Rudy narrowed his eyes. "Guinness Book of World Records."

Rudy turned and marched away.

"What did you do?" Claudia said, glaring at Stanley. She moved to follow her husband, but Stanley stopped her.

"I think I asked some valid questions," Stanley said, taking her hand more tightly this time.

"I don't want him to go for a record."

"Why? What's the difference between that and what he's doing now?"

"It's one thing to compete against other people in these competitions. There's either a time limit, or a limit to how many peppers, or he stops when he's the last man standing. But a record is just what he can eat until he can't."

"So?"

"I don't know how many that is. He's addicted. What if he doesn't stop? Or can't?"

Stanley stood on stage with the microphone in his hand. "I want to welcome everyone to this momentous occasion. My good friend and fellow pepper fiend Rudy Mayer is about to make history."

Rudy glared up at Stanley, looking about ready to murder the guy, but the crowd must have taken it for determination, his own fire to combat the inferno he was about to ingest.

"The ghost pepper," Stanley said, holding one up in a latexed hand. It goes by many names: Naga Jolokia, Naga Morich, Bih Jolokia, U-morok, ghost chili pepper, or red naga chili. The Bhut Jolokia is cultivated in the Nagaland and Assam regions of north-eastern India and parts of neighbouring Bangladesh. It has clocked in at one million Scovilles. For those not in the know, that can be twice, but is more likely ten times, as hot as a habanero. And we all know how hot that is."

Most of the crowd nodded enthusiastically, and some even whistled. These were not newbies to the world of peppers. Claudia recognized a few from previous events.

Stanley brought out two latex gloves from his pocket. "And these are so hot, my friends, that our intrepid adventurer must suit up. As it were."

Stanley held out a glove. Rudy marched toward him and for a moment Claudia worried Rudy might punch that showy smile off Stanley's face. Instead, Rudy grinned at the crowd and put the latex gloves on himself, snapping the rim with a playful grin. The crowd woo-wooed and cheered and pumped their fists.

Claudia stood near the lip of the stage. A large security man stood nearby, a barrier against the rowdy crowd pushing to get the best footage on their phones, or those so caught up in the frenzy that toes and elbows were trifling details. The Guinness Book officials stood behind Rudy, looking stern and attentive. They glanced over the table and the peppers and Rudy and then nodded at Stanley. Stanley held up his hands, and the crowd grew still and quiet.

"Time to make history," Stanley said, and Rudy lunged into action.

Claudia grasped her hands together so tightly it hurt, but the idea of letting go seemed as impossible as what she was seeing on the stage. Rudy sat, elbows resting on the table, plucking one shrivelled, shining red teardrop after another. He took the stalk in his latex-covered fingers, and munched from the tip toward the shoulder. Sometimes he bit off the flesh of the pepper with his teeth at the calyx, taking all of the pepper into his mouth, and chewed. With relish, with joy. One after another.

"He's in fine form," Stanley said, whispering into Claudia's ear.

She eyed him up and down, and leaned away before her gaze returned to her husband on the stage. Rudy glared in Stanley's direction but otherwise didn't pause in his efforts to continually funnel ghost peppers toward his mouth.

A bell rang, and the crowd erupted in cheers, but Rudy continued eating.

"What's that?" Claudia said.

"He's passed the previous record," Stanley said.

"Then why isn't he stopping?"

"He wants to crush the record. Looks like he might do it."

"This is crazy," Claudia said. "I've got to say something to him. I've got to stop him."

Claudia pushed by Stanley and made her way up the stairs. A crowd had settled in an arch around Rudy: the Guinness Book of World Records officials, the sponsors for the event, security. They made room for her but only just, and she still had to push her way past. She aimed her sights on Rudy, but as she stepped closer to him, her vision blurred. She staggered on until she stood behind him. "You've done it, Rudy," she said, leaning close to his ear.

"I know," he said, and popped another pepper in his mouth.

"You can stop."

"Why? This is easy," he said, chewing and bringing yet another pepper to his mouth. "Do you see what I'm doing?" He swallowed. "It freaked me out at first, but I can feel it." He grabbed two peppers this time. "A sort of jittery sensation. I think it's the peppers."

"Maybe you should stop if you're not feeling well," Claudia said, her breath catching in her throat as he took three peppers by their stalks and chomped through their tips.

Rudy shook his head as he polished off the three, not breaking his rhythm in the least as he waved for another bowl to be set on the table. "I'm feeling fine." He slid the empty bowl out of the way while pulling the full one to him. "They taste great."

"*Can* you taste them?"

"Yeah. It tastes like humming."

An official tapped Claudia on the shoulder, and she jerked up. "Mrs Mayer, perhaps your husband should stop."

"Is there a time limit?" Rudy asked.

"Well, not per se. It is in one sitting, but——"

"I'm still sitting," Rudy said, popping another pepper in his mouth. "So keep counting."

"Mrs Mayer. He might do irreparable damage."

"I'm still good," Rudy said. The official shrugged and stepped back.

Claudia leaned closer to her husband. The crowd was growing louder, and she was not sure he would hear her if she didn't. "Please stop, Rudy."

He popped another pepper in his mouth. "It feels like the more I eat, the easier it gets." Another pepper followed. "I think I'm burning them off as I eat them."

Claudia stared at her husband. Fear brought tears to her eyes, making her vision blur. Rudy's face grew hazy. She wiped away the tears, but though she squinted, she could not see him clearly. Claudia cast about the stage for help. There stood Stanley and the judges, the excited crowd, hands pumping the air in support. But when she turned back to her husband, to her horror, she realized it was Rudy who was becoming out of focus.

"Rudy," Claudia said, and reached to touch him on the shoulder. Her hand passed right through him. "Oh my god. Rudy." Claudia's voice was drowned out by the noise from beyond the stage.

"Big Bhut. Big Bhut. Big Bhut." The crowd chanted in time with his munching. Rudy nodded as he gazed out over the crowd. Smiling and chewing. Chewing and smiling. And slowly fading from view.

The crowd surged. Some even climbed over the lip, so eager were they to share in the marvel before them. Claudia felt herself carried away from the table and toward the wings of the stage. Her head spinning, and shock making her weak, she lost her footing and fell to her knees. The voices around her swirled, climbing octaves only to fall to a pitch so low she could feel it only as a pressure against her chest.

"Claudia. Claudia." Stanley's voice penetrated her dizziness. He helped her to her feet and away from the throng that besieged the stage. "He did it. He crushed that record. No one will ever surpass him. Did you see? Did you see?"

Claudia nodded weakly. She had. She had seen her husband disappear.

Claudia shivered as she wrapped her terry-cloth robe around herself. She leaned over the laptop and scrolled through the headlines that even a month later still peppered the internet. *Man Disappears at Eat-Off. Guinness Officials Perplexed.* One headline declared, *A Record Never To Be Broken.* Post after post, some even had Rudy's picture, but of course it was only his transit ID. There weren't any photos of him from the day. No pictures of the Big Bhut. None good enough for the news. All that was captured that day on cell phones and cameras was a blur beside empty bowls that used to contain one hundred ghost peppers.

She felt Rudy's frigid hand wind through the opening of her robe. His arm settled on her hips, and he squeezed her ass. Claudia shivered as she scrolled to the next paragraph.

Ghosts were supposed to be cold, but Rudy wasn't dead. Still, it was strange to feel his touch against her cool skin without seeing him there. The cold showers were bracing, but they seemed to help. Over time, Rudy was becoming more corporeal, more present. And if that was the only way they could be together, then that's the way it would have to be. They both had to make sacrifices.

A slight change in air pressure, and his presence rose out of the chair. If she squinted, she could see his wavering outline as it moved past the sink and the blender, the glass tinted blue from her most recent recipe. It moved past the stove that held a pot of her spaghetti sauce and the two dozen jars on the counter for canning. *Big Bhut Bolognese.*

Rudy continued until he stood at the opposite end of the kitchen table. Where once a bowl of peppers sat, there was a bowl filled with ice surrounding a gigantic blue-raspberry slushie. The slushie was already half-finished. No more heat for the Big Bhut. Chilling the outside and the inside was the only thing that helped his condition.

Claudia peered at the top of the straw. "Keep going, babe," Claudia said. "You're doing great."

The straw moved, and the slushie level sank down to a third. The outline of her husband's face came into focus as he winced and held his head. Brain freeze.

"Hey," Claudia said. "I can see you."

HEAVEN OR LAS VEGAS

Paige Elizabeth Wajda

Paige Elizabeth Wajda *is from California. She spent four years teaching English in Poland before earning a master's degree in Creative Writing from the University of Edinburgh. Her work has recently appeared in* The London Reader, Red Planet Magazine, *and* Impossible Archetype, *and in 2020 she was awarded a Keep Art Alive grant from the California Desert Arts Council. Find her online at paigeelizabethwords.wordpress.com.*

$\mathcal{H}$EAVEN OR LAS VEGAS

Night drive. The all-hail moon gobbles me
down. A lover lingers on the edge of my shirt:
sunburn and hickeys contend upon my neck.

On the oldies station, a Scottish Elizabeth
sings of Las Vegas sun across time
and space.

I have stood on both ends of the Earth.
Now, somewhere in the desert I drive on, singing
alongside this supermoon.

It glowers, making sure I use my turn signals.
I glow at the speed of cruising altitude.

Fine arm-hairs surge up with sound-fever, I forget
the sweat sticking to my globs, squashed by the seatbelt,
in a dream at the derelict intersection. The light

turns green. Bare-ankled in my silver-apple pickup,
I press down: on gravity-light lunar surfaces,
I drive with a leadfoot.

THE EARTH HAS BUBBLES

PG Streeter

PG Streeter lives with his wife and two sons in Maryland, where he teaches high school English and philosophy. His previous publications include work in Daily Science Fiction, StarShipSofa, and Electric Spec. 'The Earth Has Bubbles' takes its title and a good deal of inspiration from William Shakespeare's Macbeth.

The Earth Has Bubbles

With him I marched across heath and moor, as soil and blood caked our boots and swords. I marched with him through the rebels' ranks, and we waded through heaps of dead men, much as we'd trudged through marsh and bog, day upon day during that long march. We stood together and did bloody battle, and later they sang of us as twin cannons cracking—

—but that is just the way of songs. Really, there was little poetry in it: we earned every inch of our passage with swinging sword and ever-plodding foot, and men did not quail before us but met us with the possessed strength that such occasions bring. The sounds of battle, of our swords rending flesh and bone, were not like thunder-crash or cannonade. If you have not heard the sound of a blade running a man through, or of a spine being severed, or of a soldier's final, gurgling death-cry, I count you blessed; I will not ask you to hear such sounds today.

I am a skilled horseman, of course — as is he — and as generals under Donnchad's banner we oft rode ahead on horse, our Lord's light cavalry and heavy infantry filing behind us. The horses never lasted, though; all our company was on foot long before that final confrontation. How many of those miles did we tread upon our own worn leather boots?

With him I must have walked across all of Scotland.

Son of Findláech: by our swelling feet, we were brothers.

On my last day—after battle had ended, and I believed, for a moment, the lie of peace—I rode, and my son rode at my side. But we dismounted and were treading lightly afoot when the cutthroats, hired men cloaked in hood and shadow, fell upon us.

So it is on foot that I now continue to stride across this blasted land.

My son does not walk with me, and this gives me courage: either he fled and lives, or, dying, fled *elsewhere*. May he find himself in fields lit by the cool sun of early autumn. I can hope.

But it shames me to admit that I did not look for my boy afterward. I simply stood up and looked down and saw myself heaped in a ditch—a trench riven amongst grey rock and gnarled root—and began to walk. While I lived, my last cries had been for my son—for his flight from that accursed spot—but in death, in stepping out of my flesh and into shadow, I cared only about *him*. Not my boy, but the Red King. I will not say his name.

I stepped out of flesh and walked as a shade upon the heath until Forres emerged from fog and stood backlit by the setting sun. I saw it all as if through a veil, and none who passed me on the road perceived me. But the Sisters are beings of that same shadow, and they now walked with me, although I could not see them.

They whispered.

You will get kings, the first said, but this was nothing new. It might have warmed my heart if I'd still had one, for it was proof of my only son's survival, and of his sons to come.

Yet it gave me no peace, and I walked.

Lesser and greater, the second said, *did we not say it was so? Noble thane. Man of trust. So easily bested — but are you not comforted to know your part was the better? To know you did not fall from grace as he did?*

I was not, and I suspect she knew this.

Then: *Go now*, the third said, *for your place is prepared, and you are the guest of honour.* This was new, and I walked forward, ever listening. *Your seat awaits, and the feast is not yet begun, and we three can unfold the air and reveal you to his eyes, for just a moment. It will be enough.*

"The earth has bubbles," I said aloud, repeating something I'd said to him mere days before. The Sisters laughed, and then their shrill voices trailed off, and then I walked alone.

It was as the Sisters said. I walked into the king's hall and took my appointed seat at the banquet, and the Sisters unveiled me to his eyes alone. I did not speak words, but in this shared space — for we both stood within a pocket of the world — thoughts passed between us without speech.

Without speaking, I said, *You killed me, you bastard.*

I had rehearsed my speech to him all along my walk from my shallow grave; this, in the end, was all I could compose. The words were apt enough.

The Red King was taken aback, and though he needed but think and I would hear, he bellowed loudly, "Let the earth hide thee!" He did not see, as I now did: the earth indeed hid me, at least to all other eyes. And it hid part of him as well, though he knew it not. He continued to cry out, and all could hear his protestations, that the thing so plain before him simply could not be.

So droned his feeble-minded pleas while I remained silent. I knew that, just as I was unveiled to him, he was now unveiled to the lords and ladies gathered before him. I suppressed a grin.

And, after a time, I silenced him with mere thought: *You king of rats*, my mind spoke to him. *A rat dressed as a man dressed as a king. I see your guise: robes and coronet sit upon skin and brow, but your very skin is itself a garment of manlike flesh, dressing something . . . less.*

There we were, pocketed in that space. Our environs appeared to be a gilded hall, but where we stood was, in truth, somewhere . . . *between*—between bone and skin, perhaps? Or: he was a step down a great stair from living, I, a step up from death. We met in the middle.

Again and again he bid me be gone, but I saw that he carried this place with him—this *in-between,* a folding of the world around him wherever he tread—and still he did not know it. So I crawled in.

Under robe, under flesh, deep as bone but not bone.

In that under-space, I found that I was not alone.

My Liege Lord awaited me there, and we were blended and mingled now so that I could hardly tell where he ended and I began. My faculties strained to keep either of us apart from the other—and from the thing in man-shape whose shadowed mind we now inhabited. I played tricks of thought to stay alive.

For instance: I pictured myself a scorpion. My vengeance was its piercing tail, and it prodded ever at this imposter's mind, this player king. I stung at him and stung again, but the venom was his own, and I drew into my tail like ink into a quill, merely redistributing what was already there. I prayed (to whom? to the Sisters? no God would hear me now) that it did him sufficient malice.

Others joined as time passed: a woman and her babes, now spectral and enfolded here in bitterness with the rest of us. And soon, more: servants and courtiers alike crowded here, in this place that was no place. We were all one, and we were all a part of him.

As days unfurled into weeks, we found ourselves diminishing, but as we did — as our world came closer to the full shadow for which we knew we must be bound — he became closer to us, and we to him.

In the end, he knew us and therefore knew himself. As the forest rose to swallow him, just before he was ripped from the world, my thoughts became his, and he spoke them aloud.

I thought of the day I died and awoke to trudge across the fields and hillocks to his door. I envisioned the veiled march through the dead grass, and he uttered, "Life is but a walking shadow." The images continued to unfold before me, and he said, "A poor player" — here he paused, groaned, and finished with effort through parched lips — "who struts and frets his hour upon the stage …"

His spirit walked with me now along that heath, and as his body stood still in anticipation of some final battle, the sounds of the world — even of his own voice — grew distant. There was a muffled din of crashing and shouting, but its meaning could take no shape. He turned to me, and, his visage contorting in anguish, parted his lips to speak.

But the world began to lose all form —

— and popped.

LIFE SUPPORTS

Claire Lawrence

Claire Lawrence is a storyteller and mixed-media visual artist living in British Columbia, Canada. She has been published in Canada, the United States, the United Kingdom, Germany, and India. Her work has been performed on BBC Radio. Claire's stories have appeared in numerous publications including Geist, Litro, Ravensperch, Brilliant Flash Fiction, Hot Flash Fiction, *and more. She has a number of prize-winning stories, and was nominated for the 2016 Pushcart Prize. Claire's artwork has appeared in many magazines including* A3 Review and Press, Cold Mountain Review, Inverted Syntax, Black Lion Journal, Sunspot, *and many more. Her goal is to create and publish in all genres, and not inhale too many fumes.*

$\mathcal{L}$IFE SUPPORTS

The music starts. Glenn Miller and his orchestra playing "A String of Pearls." It's too loud, but the hard-of-hearing crowd is lulled. A woman pulls out a hanky and waves it about, surrendering to the war tune. I knew this would be a trigger. Mine will be the 1980s song 'Time After Time' by Cyndi Lauper. Jared and I used to slow-dance to it in tight circles. When he proposed and I accepted, he hugged me and cried on my shoulder. Where did those dreamy people go? My eyes get glassy, and I pinch myself to keep it together.

The screen behind me lights up. I welcome all attending, recognizing one face, and she has Alzheimer's. Her care aide is directing her attention to the photo behind me. It's a thin crowd, half a dozen if I include the care aide. I called every number in Auntie's worn-out address book. There were many dead rings.

I made the right decision to leave the boys with supper, a warm bottle, and unlimited screen time for the eldest. Besides, hubby was glued to some football championship. Why would he want to sit through this? It's a relief they're not here. I'm sure they would have survived the ceremony, but what if they listened? What if Jared understood?

I tap my index cards. Cookie dough is stuck to one corner. I flick it off, clear my throat, and begin.

"Rationing during the war freed women of steel-support corsets and rubber girdles. It changed how brassieres were designed and made. The longline coverage over the torso was shortened to an under-bust band. Pointy, unsized, full-coverage cups, sewn horizontally, were flimsy and unpadded. At the sternum, material was added, forcing the breasts to separate. In short, the newly designed undergarment became a war bra."

My opening remarks are met with watery eyes and denture play. A few old gals squawk. "What'd she say? Why's she talking about bras? Seems a bit disrespectful."

The unruliness of a few sets the others off.

"Please bear with me," I plead. "I know this is an unconventional beginning . . ."

Bang! I jump. Heads turn to the back of the room.

A gentleman, the only gentleman, has wrestled and thumped the maple door into submission with his walker. He's dressed in a faded, loose-fitting, green uniform. A matching beret sits askew on threads of white hair. He inches his way towards the front. It will take forever for him to sit. I continue.

"The first patented brassiere was granted to Mary Phelps Jacobs on November 3, 1914, by the United States Patent and Trademark Office. However, women have bound and supported their bosoms since the age of the Greeks."

Should I shut up and herd everyone towards the tea and sandwiches I made? Glancing at Auntie, seeing the slight grin on her face, I proceed, based on her mantra, "Who the heck needs to live by the status quo? I had to get by without it." This mantra emerged once her social graces and filters broke down.

The old fella is ordering a woman to move over. She's sitting in his chair. A spat erupts. Thanks to children, I've learned to let minor disputes play out. I stop, shuffle my flash cards and take a sip of water. My shoe taps a small open box by my feet. I brought memorabilia: a 1941 homemade cotton bra along with some photos I will display later. The white bra, yellowed at the armpits, has frayed straps and a faded rose clinging to the centre. On the inside of the back strap, the name Eugenia Hillsbury has been embroidered. This bra, according to Auntie, was the main reason she failed to capture a husband during the war.

"Tell him I was here first!" shouts the planted woman with balloon-dog legs.

"This seat had a reserved sign on it, and you moved it." The veteran waggles his finger at her forehead.

Maybe I should have put the sepia photograph on the screen first? I pluck it from the box. This group could relate to eighteen-year-old Auntie volunteering at the dance hall canteen, back in '41. The photo is blurred on the right. Auntie is posing in front of the counter with some fella.

"Handsome he was. A fine gentleman who respected me." Her voice would drop in disappointment whenever she repeated this tale. Yes, they danced, and even kissed. He was sweet, and asked to be introduced to her family.

"He didn't know what he was asking. I had no father. And my mother was stricter than Queen Victoria."

A tea was organized nevertheless. Auntie had to wear a dress her mother made. It was dreadfully honest. She begged her mother to let her make adjustments, but she refused. The tea was a disaster.

Her beau left her high and dry. Auntie swears that if she had been able to make embellishments, like makeup and a sock, and use a shaver, maybe her man would have stayed.

Patting down my blouse, I curse our shared DNA. Soon, all will be remedied. In two weeks I'll go under the knife. Should I tell Jared I'm going for Ds instead of Cs?

Crash.

The old fella shouts, "Don't you try and hit me, you scallywag. I was in the war," and he lifts his overturned walker.

"Get the management," screeches an elderly woman wearing a shabby bonnet.

I sigh and look to Auntie. Her white hair swoops over her head, Marilyn Monroe style. Someone did her makeup, including eyeliner and coral lipstick. She looks uptown, not her usual Reno self. Too bad. I like eye glitter.

The war photo slips from my fingers and lands on the floor. Young Auntie stares up at me with a comprehending face tucked under a cap of dark hair. Two button eyes, slightly askew, gaze out from under crescent eyebrows. She had a nose and string lips. She was passable. Any Joe might have taken to her. I pick her up, and my eye scrolls to her figure. She's dressed in a tight sleeveless knit sweater and an A-line skirt, with a jacket tossed over her shoulder. You couldn't miss her unique silhouette, highlighted by the unfortunate custom-made bra.

The flimsy support cupped and separated her breasts into two camps. The right breast, large and droopy, hung by her ribs and was topped by a good tuft of armpit hair. The left, a small precancerous mound, stuck to her chest like a barnacle. Her mother made the bra to fit.

"The popular lads wanted girls built like Rita Hayworth," she had sighed.

"They still do," I added, showing her a modern Hollywood family in a fashion magazine.

When the war ended, Auntie was single, with no babe on her hip like her friends. Her mother comforted her by saying, "All the good men died."

"I knew that wasn't true." Auntie patted my hand. "But what could I do? Without the freedom to go out, I had to live with my mother."

The seating area erupts into a full-fledged war. The gentleman has a small squad of nonnies crying for justice. Some probably hope the handsome soldier will go sweet on them.

"He reserved the seat!" they shout.

The offending woman, solid as a tank, remains planted. I roll my eyes. I don't want to break them up. Where's the director or assistant when you need them?

I glance over at Auntie. She doesn't care about the brouhaha. She's experienced enough disappointment and drama in her life, poor woman. Gutted of essentials at age thirty-one — collateral damage from pesticide on the family farm.

I can hear her saying, "I lost my mother, uterus, and breast in the same year. I was ready to give up, but then I saw Starlet."

Starlet was a bullet bra she purchased for $2.50 in 1953. "That's $19.22 in today's money," she whispered to me last week.

She's wearing it today. The blue rayon bra with taffeta trim rests on her bony, level chest, under a peach chiffon dress. There was no point in telling her that, even in today's dollars, it was a cheap bra. Yet, with her hand-washing and reinforcing the cheap elastic, it's withstood the years.

"If I'd had this bra back at the canteen," she'd tell me, "my life would have turned out differently."

The bullet bra, designed to unite, support, and elevate the bosom, was the James Bond of bras. Anything was possible in a bullet bra. After my surgery, I plan to get one.

Auntie said the bullet bra gave her confidence and direction. While women of her generation were pumping out roast beef and mashed potatoes, she got a job as a dealer in Reno.

"I stuffed Starlet with a wad of cotton, got myself a pink Remington shaver, platinum hair, and spray-on makeup. I had men hanging off me."

The old folks' bickering has been going on too long. I tap the microphone.

"I'd like to get started."

Nope, no one's listening. I feel like I haven't left home, what with the fighting and noxious smells of stale urine and poopy pants. I shouldn't complain. My unshaved armpits, in this polyester blouse, are reeking. I was in such a rush to escape the house, I forgot to shower and put on deodorant. Why didn't Jared say something?

No matter. Soon I'm going to burn every frumpy blouse I own and get sexy bras. It'll be liberating.

The thought of enhancing my wardrobe makes me think of Auntie's forbidden closet. She used to keep it locked. Yesterday, I entered her lair of exotic wares and discovered a whole new lifestyle. I didn't know how half the stuff worked. It gave me ideas.

"Sir. Ma'am." The director has arrived. He's calming the crowd with a smooth, hushed voice, coaxing most back to the chairs. The veteran is adamant about his spot. The director looks to me. I shrug. He eyes his watch and whispers into the old man's ear before heading to the back of the room.

Goodness, he's got a tight ass.

My fantasy of him taking me on the reception table ends when Jared and the boys enter and sit quietly at the back. My husband gives me a warm, supportive smile, and holds up a fresh blouse on a hanger. Our little guy is in the crook of his other arm.

My lip quivers. Seeing them reminds me of my last conversation with Auntie.

"Any regrets?" I asked her.

Her breath was raspy and strained, and her grip on my hand was cold.

"I wish I could have had a family of my own. Not that you aren't like a daughter to me, dear. But you know what I mean, to have a life like yours."

"My life is caring for whiny, snotty kids. Half the time I have spit-up and stains on me. And Jared and I have plain vanilla sex. Who would want that?"

She smiled and gave me the key to her closet. "Take what you want."

"Hi, Mommy," yells Matthew, standing on his chair. He's dressed in a little three-piece suit. Where did he get that? The penny drops. Jared shopped for it before the service. He planned to be here all along.

The director returns. My fantasy man has hair stuck to his oversized forehead, and his glasses are sliding down his nose. He's struggling to carry a metal chair. My eye twitches. The old soldier follows him to the front.

Yesterday, after sifting through Auntie's chest of drawers, I discovered every bra she had ever bought. They were dated and wrapped in tissue. Her life was lived through every padded, underwire, lace, peek-a-boo, and studded-leather bra. I thought it would be clever to recount Auntie's unconventional life through her lingerie. Now I'm having doubts.

The cane, wheelchair, and walker folk settle. The director has placed the veteran in a special spot: beside Auntie. He's having a loud chat with her.

"Darling Eugenia, you look as beautiful as ever. It's Howard. I don't suppose you remember me? It's been a long time, hasn't it? I wanted to come by and share my respects. I'm curious, did you ever marry? After your dreadful mother sent me away for not being good enough, I had to marry Hillary, if you know what I mean. It's a terrible thing to say, but I wasn't in love with her."

He pauses and sighs. When he speaks again, his voice warbles and tears roll down his cheeks.

"I want you to know I thought of you every day. Promise me you'll greet me when I join you on the other side."

I set my cards aside.

The music begins again. The screen lights up with an image of wartime Auntie. She's dressed in her sleeveless, knitted sweater. The strap of her homemade bra peeks out. She's giving the camera the sweetest smile.

Howard hauls himself up and blows a kiss to the screen.

Jared gives me the thumbs-up. The baby blows milk bubbles. Matthew is bouncing. Everyone is waiting.

I realize I've got this all wrong, even Auntie's life. I swallow, adjust my blouse, and wing it.

"Dear family and friends, thank you for attending Eugenia Hillsbury's celebration of life. What a woman!

"Auntie was blessed with a long and lively life, but certain events changed the course of her destiny. She faced each hurdle with courage, including her battle with cancer. I want you to know you were integral to her life. You were her supports in times of need. Thank you for honouring her."

I hear purses snapping open.

The gentleman puts a hand on his heart, leans over the casket, and says goodbye to Auntie. Then he grabs his walker and heads for the exit.

The clutch of women follow his cue. They rise and pay their respects, and shuffle out.

I look to my husband. He blows me a kiss.

THE SMELL OF SCREAMING

Adrienne Gruber

Adrienne Gruber is the author of three books of poetry — Q & A (Book*hug), Buoyancy Control (Book*hug), and This Is the Nightmare (Thistledown Press) — and five chapbooks. Her chapbook Mimic was awarded the bpNichol Chapbook Award in 2012. Adrienne lives in Vancouver with her partner and three daughters. 'The Smell of Screaming' received an Honourable Mention for the 2020 Surrey International Writers' Conference Storyteller's Award.

The Smell of Screaming

Inhale

When Granny moved into my parents' house, my mom renovated the upstairs bedroom and moved my dad's office into the basement. Mom ripped up the carpet and put in laminate flooring. She painted the walls eggshell and had a new window installed. The old one that I used to sneak out of as a teenager was discarded. Granny's antique furniture was shipped from Ontario, where she had been living with my aunt for the last decade.

The sense of smell comes about through the stimulation of specialized cells in a body's nasal cavities — cells that are similar to the sensory cells of the antennæ of invertebrates. The human olfactory system works when odorant molecules bind to specific sites on the olfactory receptors, which are used to detect the presence of smell.

Over the years that Granny lived with my parents, routines were formed. She'd shuffle into the kitchen with her walker an hour before noon, demanding to know when lunch was served.

She'd remind my mom how she took her coffee —"One third coffee, two thirds cream"— as if my mom hadn't been putting out the same egg salad sandwich and fruit cup and preparing her coffee for the last thousand days.

It all comes together at the glomerulus, a structure that transmits signals to the olfactory bulb —a part of the brain directly above the nasal cavity and below the frontal lobe. The end result is the subjective experience we call smell.

Granny drove us all nuts with her demands and barking orders, her moodiness, her obsessive rituals. Her social interactions were a series of repetitive questions usually directed at my dad, who'd watch sports in the living room as she ate her meals. *Where is that game taking place, Klaus? What type of sport is that? Who's winning?* Questions ran on a continuous loop for each person in her life. Her dementia worsened with every year.

When I came home to visit, I swear I could smell it.

While the human nose can detect over a trillion smells, there are about ten basic categories of odours that are systematically used for describing smells:

1. **Fruity** *(all non-citrus fruits)*

When I tell my workshopping group I want to write about bodies from the perspective of smell, there's an awkward silence. Our instructor finally says, "Yes, that's an avenue not many have explored."

I didn't get what she meant until later —no one really wants to contemplate how the human body smells. Especially with aging. With mental illness. In women's bodies. In pregnancy. In menstruation. In sex. In hormonal shifts. In humanity. No one wants to think too hard about armpits. Genitalia. Feet. Or the odours that emerge when you're gestating a human. Or when you're in the thick of menopause and you're bleeding endlessly or soaking shirts with your own sweat.

Capitalism has its hooks in smell, using the term *scent branding*—associating a scent with a brand—to create a closer bond with consumers. Customers will recall the brand or product when they smell the scent. These scent logos, as they're sometimes called, embody unique brand characteristics. After all, consumers are happy to think of the baby powder smell of a slender neck or soft freckled shoulder in summer. Hair, if you wash regularly. The parts of you that can transform into man-made fragrance.

I didn't used to have a great sense of smell. It was handy when I had cats; the litter box never bothered me. If I walked past a particularly smelly bin of garbage it wouldn't make my stomach heave. Over time and three pregnancies, I've developed hyperosmia, a heightened sense of smell. My threshold for odour has decreased dramatically, and I seem to be smelling everything.

Apparently, a decline in one's sense of smell is an early marker of mild cognitive impairment.

I remember the smell of my granny's bedroom in my parents' house—stale Arrowroot biscuits, mothballs. Dead air. Fermented flesh.

2. **Citrus** *(e.g. lemon, lime, orange)*

I'm unaffected by desirable smells and completely repulsed by anything else. It feels like a window into the next stage of life, where bodies emit their slow decay. I'm triggered by these odours, angered by the injustice of having to smell them.

I've started inhaling citrus to remind myself of vibrancy, of a body that's alive.

Researchers can use olfactory tests to predict one's likelihood of developing dementia. In one study, participants had to identify five odours, one at a time, by sniffing a device that resembled a felt-tip pen, like the smelly markers my daughters love to inhale. Cherry, blueberry, lemon. Toasted marshmallow. Black liquorice. All those candy smells, that sticky sweetness.

The five odours in the study were peppermint, fish, orange, rose, and leather. Peppermint was considered the easiest to identify and leather the hardest. I can't imagine going back to colouring after smelling a fish-scented pen.

3. *Woody and resinous* (e.g. pine, fresh cut grass)

After almost a decade of Granny living with my parents, she was moved into a care home, and my parents moved out to Vancouver to be close to my family. They brought my granny's old antique furniture with them—the smell of those lost years of care imprinted on the vintage fabric and stained wood.

I learned recently that the smell of freshly cut grass is actually the smell of a number of volatile organic compounds called green leaf volatiles (GLVs) that are released when the grass is damaged. Anything can cause widespread damage: insects, grazing animals, unintentional rough handling. Infections too, or mechanical forces—like a lawnmower. That delightful smell of a freshly cut lawn is the grass trying to save itself from injury. It's a distress signal. Some of the compounds released stimulate the formation of new cells at the site of the wound so it closes faster. Others act as antibiotics to prevent infection in the plant. The rush of chemicals emitted into the air (what we breathe in deeply and satisfyingly, known as 'green' odour) creates healing possibilities. However, regardless of the preventative measures that are the result of these compounds, it's a cry for help. The result of fresh trauma.

In other words, it is the smell of grass screaming in pain.

I think we must smell the most alive when we're in the most vibrant pain. It's when we're numbed or subdued or broken—but functional—that we stop leaving a scent trail.

4. *Chemical* (*e.g. ammonia, bleach*)

Bodily scents are not taken into account in the ten basic odours. Bodies and their slow, stagnant decline.

As her dementia deepened, my granny refused to allow caregivers to help her bathe. My mom scheduled a health-care worker to come and give her a bath twice a week, and my granny called the agency and cancelled every appointment.

I take one or two showers a day, depending on the weather and how physically active I've been. When I'm pregnant, I shower as many as three times a day. My own seasoned aroma seeps through my underwear almost as quickly as I can dress myself after. Gestational hormonal shifts turn bodies into petri dishes.

At some point in Granny's early years of living with my parents, my mom discovered that Granny had been cleaning her vagina with hydrogen peroxide during the daily sponge baths she'd give herself at the bathroom sink. Whether it was compulsive hygiene or more of a purification ritual, the bleach began to eat away at the enamel over time. The slow corrosion resulted in my parents having to replace the sink before selling their house.

5. *Fragrant (e.g. florals, perfumes)*

I had a disastrous Brazilian wax during my first pregnancy. I wanted a break from the hair that matted in the damp tent of my underwear. I lay on the cot, with my legs splayed as the æsthetician decorated me with hot wax, and immediately knew it was a mistake. I didn't know that pregnancy increased blood flow to the skin's surface, resulting in highly sensitive skin. What I *did* know was that the wax had to come off. She was quick, flicking her wrist away from the hair growth, but the pain was an immediate ringing in my ears, like the screaming of shredded grass.

I don't feel so great, I muttered, which was code for *I'm either going to faint, vomit, or shit myself on this cot.* I sat up and put my head between my knees, hoping the wax wouldn't stick to other parts of me. The æsthetician left the room without a word and returned with a glass of ice water. The wax smelled like honey, with floral notes and butterscotch. I imagined a cluster of bees swarming my half-bald vulva, searching for nectar to take back to the hive.

6. *Sweet (e.g. chocolate, vanilla, caramel)*

Though I have never fully understood this, the scent of newborn heads seems to trigger bliss in people. So many suggest fresh milky-sweet innocence. Can innocence have a smell? Probably, but I doubt it comes in the form of a head that's barrelled out of a vaginal canal, or through the layers of muscle and fat of a torso. When I inhale a newborn crown, all I smell is an unwashed, slightly sour odour. Spit-up resin. The waxy remnants of cradle cap. I can smell the post-partum exhaustion.

When I was a teenager, whenever my mom hugged me, she would breathe me in and whisper, *you smell so good*. I never quite understood what the smell of my skin did for her, though I would swoon a bit from feeling that I had been so intoxicating to someone else. It was only when I had my own daughters and started smelling them that I understood how mothers need to breathe in their children. It's like burrowing your face in fresh earth. My children's stink makes me instantly drunk. Their teeth, when they haven't been brushed in days, that smell of fermented fruit and granola bars. Their sun-bleached hair from hours of rolling in the sand at the beach, dried salt tangled in their briny scalps.

It is different from the smell of newborn heads. It's not that I don't appreciate the scent; it's more that I don't smell what others seem to. My newborns always smelled like me, like the ocean that regenerates itself from both the dead and the living sea creatures that make up its body.

7. ***Minty and peppermint*** *(e.g. eucalyptus, camphor)*

Memory is likely more closely linked to your sense of smell than to any of your other senses.

My daughters bring me mint and basil from our patio garden. They make 'summer drinks' where they pour glasses of bubbly water and add frozen fruit and dozens of mint leaves. I can see their hair grow, almost daily, and I smell the cells in their small bodies multiplying at rapid rates, healing scrapes and bruises quickly and efficiently. They bathe twice a week at the most, less so in the summer, and somehow their bodies always smell like flowers and freshly butchered grass. The smell of fresh screaming. Of shrieks of joy.

There aren't many smells that pull memories back into my consciousness. In fact, I have a terrible memory.

I can't remember what my mother smelled like when I was growing up. I'm trying.

8 . **Toasted and nutty** *(e.g. popcorn, peanut butter, almonds)*

I used to go home to Saskatoon for extended visits in the summer and answer my own loop of questions from Granny: *Where do you live again, Adrienne? What does your husband do? How long have you been married? How many kids do you want? Have I ever given you an afghan?*

I have several afghans, most of which are stored in the space under the sectional in my living room and have a permanent musty smell. Others were given away to old roommates. My sixteen cousins and I have all received multiple afghans over the years, for birthdays and weddings and sometimes just because. The afghans were strangely perfect for movie watching. I would bundle myself up in two or three, then let my bare toes poke through the holes, a large bowl of heavily buttered popcorn in my lap.

9 . **Pungent** *(e.g. blue cheese, cigar smoke)*

Decades before she lived with my parents, and shortly after my granddad died of a heart attack in the bathtub, Granny moved in with her sister, my great-aunt Kay. After two years of Granny's demands and tantrums, Kay kicked her out and refused to have anything to do with her. Granny moved in with my Aunt Jackie and lived in the suite over the garage for the next decade.

She smoked in the suite, and the smell reminded me of when I was a kid and would visit my grandparent's Victorian-looking apartment, where Granddad would sit in his underwear, smoking and reading the paper. I don't remember him interacting with me at all, but there are photos of me when I was about six, with a bowl haircut and brown corduroy overalls, climbing all over him and laughing. He is smiling in the photos. I'm grateful for the documentation. Without it, the only thing I remember is the thick smell of smoke.

At Grandad's funeral, Granny seemed petrified of her own grief. She instructed her daughters and grandchildren that we were under no circumstances allowed to cry at the service. I was eight. My mother and aunts told their mother that she was not allowed to dictate how they grieved for their father. It came out later that Granddad had numerous debts he'd kept from Granny. Devastated by the loss, and overwhelmed by the financial burden, she tried to throw out or burn memories of him and their life together. She sold the family cottage at Sand Lake and instructed my mom and aunts to take boxes of photo albums to the dump. My mom promised they would. Later, my mom and her sisters divided up the memorabilia from the two boxes my mom stashed in her car — photos and letters from their parents' love story — making sure Granny never knew.

I can smell those burning boxes in my sleep. I can smell my mom's tears. I can smell the musty interior of the Sand Lake cottage, the fresh cold of the lake. Leeches sometimes attached to us when we swam, sucking down our warm, copper-smelling blood.

*10. **Decayed** (e.g. rotting meat, sour milk)*

My husband makes a roast chicken one night a few months into my third pregnancy, and I leave the apartment for two hours because the smell (and the idea of the smell) of an oil-slicked, rosemary-stuffed dead bird makes me retch.

Hormones marinating inside of me pour out every night, and I wake dripping with sweat. Droplets of fluid slide down my chest and arms, down the back of my neck as though I'd just stepped out of the shower. I lay a towel down on the wet sheet and go back to sleep, then wake up an hour later, having soaked through the towel.

When the sheets dry they smell like a salt bed after the tide has retreated. Bacteria multiply and break down into an acidic pool, seventy-five per cent contained in the beaker of my body during the day, then flood the sheets each night.

A baby will be born soon. She'll attach herself to the outside of my body and suck the milk from my breasts, leaving me soured as she satiates.

Exhale

It's summer, and I'm nine months pregnant, so smells come stronger—the good and the bad. I detect the slow death of bodies, even as I am growing a new one. Perhaps *because* I am growing a new one. Even my own body smells of sacrifice.

Granny was ninety-one when she was finally placed in the care facility. I saw her once before she died. Miraculously, she still knew who I was, though she couldn't remember to whom I belonged.

I hugged her frail skeleton. She smelled of nothing. She smelled of a mind gone, content in its departure.

I can't hug my own mother, who has stopped showering, whose musk encroaches on me and makes my stomach churn. For months, I have hoped she would realize this on her own.

Everything outside is fragrant and bursting with life.

THE RAVEN SHORT STORY CONTEST

THE RAVEN SHORT STORY CONTEST

Captivating and radiant, the 2020 Raven Short Story Contest submissions offered an incredible range of voices and well-written prose. Thank you to all submitting authors for sharing your marvellous words and supporting Pulp Literature Press.

We would like to thank this year's judge, Matthew Hughes, who is a freshly crowned winner himself. He became the first ever Canadian to win the Endeavour Award for his novel *What the Wind Brings*, which we are extremely chuffed to have published. Here's what Matthew had to say about the winner and runner-up:

First Place: Nancy Ludmerer for 'Good Intentions'
The prose is strong and so is the narrative tension.

Honourable Mention: Erin MacNair for 'It Can Be Done with Words'
Matthew praised this story for its *imaginative concept.*

Editors' Choice: Sarina Bosco for 'Come Back Around'
We editors refuse to settle for just one literary love and couldn't resist the siren song of 'Come Back Around'. With stunning prose and chilling imagery, this story captivated us with its haunting call.

This year's shortlist, in alphabetical order:

Sarina Bosco, 'Come Back Around'
Laura Kuhlmann, 'Hear the Colours'
Nancy Ludmerer, 'Good Intentions'
Erin MacNair, 'It Can Be Done With Words'
Krista Jane May, 'Someone Knows'
Robert Runte, 'The Library Custodian'
Megan W Shaw, 'The Wild Rose'
Pam Watts, 'The Maestro'

Nancy Ludmerer *has fiction in* Kenyon Review, Carve *(where her story 'A Simple Case' won Carve's 2019 Prose & Poetry Contest),* Electric Literature, The Saturday Evening Post, Litro, *and other places. Her flash fiction has been reprinted in* Best Small Fictions, *translated into Spanish, and read aloud on NPR-affiliated radio, and her short memoir 'Kritios Boy' (Literal Latte) was named a notable essay in* Best American Essays 2014. *Most recently, her story 'Matchbox' won second prize in the* Masters Review's *summer contest. She lives in New York City, where she practised law for many years before turning to writing full-time.*

Erin MacNair *is a writer from North Vancouver, BC. She's published in* The Walrus, Room, The Feathertale Review, EVENT, *and has a forthcoming story in* Prairie Fire. *She's working on a book of short stories and a novel, and she occasionally pens a blog,* Views from the Obtuse Angle.

$\mathcal{G}$ood Intentions

by Nancy Ludmerer

When Drew announced our move and promised Hanna a dog, his intentions were good. He speculated that a six-year-old would mourn the mid-year loss of her school and her friends as much as I mourned leaving *my* job and *my* friend, who really was just a friend, no matter what Drew suspected. But when Hanna crept downstairs to the chilly living room of our new home on Christmas morning, she found, instead of a puppy, two hamsters hard at work, noses to the wheel. They looked like twins, each in his cage — to avoid squabbles, according to the pet store guy. He had shown Drew a whitish mark like a number eight on one hamster's forehead; that one was Henry the Eighth. The other hamster, Roy, screwed up his face a lot, which made him look owlish.

Hanna was an exceptionally polite child. She hid her disappointment. When she asked who Henry the Eighth was, Drew said, "a guy, a king, with a lot of wives." That evening, after Hanna was in bed, Drew said, "See? That wasn't so bad."

When I got up later and shuffled into the hall in my flannel bathrobe and wool socks to pee, I heard her sniffling in her room. She was girded by stuffed animals on all sides. No bears, no rabbits, no kangas, lambs, or kittens. Only dogs: Snoopy, Lassie, Scooby-Doo, McDuff, and a velveteen dachsie that Drew referred to disparagingly as 'sausage dog' and pretended to eat with mustard, causing Hanna, in happier times, to scream with delight and dismay.

The same way Drew craved a house in the country, Hanna craved a dog. But when it came to it, Drew decided puppies were natural-born homewreckers. Not that he loved hamsters. "They're slightly disgusting, aren't they?" he commented, a few weeks after Christmas. One morning, the hamsters' cages had been moved to the basement. "Out of sight, out of mind," Drew said cheerfully.

Hanna adjusted; she compartmentalized her life in a way that seemed overly mature for a six-year-old, and that reminded me of myself. When she came home from school, she'd visit the hamsters and talk baby talk to them. She organized their food — "Eat your veggies!" she commanded — and took them from their cages for stroking. Sometimes she listened to their hearts. Along with instructions for making the hamsters comfortable in their new home came a checklist of hamster ailments. We reviewed them together. Hanna checked each hamster's well-being regularly: "Sneezing — no; diarrhœa — no; pink eye — no; aimless circling" — which indicated an ear infection — "no."

Drew viewed Hanna's engagement with the hamsters as proof he'd made a good choice. "She's learning things," he said. "Being responsible. Now my only worry is having to pay for veterinary school. What is it, six years?" He was kidding, but not kidding.

He couldn't help it, his mind always working like that, an endless stream of cost-benefit analysis. Same thing with my job, the job I loved, the job I laboured so hard to get: Assistant DA, Kings County, aka Brooklyn, New York. For Drew, the suspicions aroused by my closeness with my team leader, my hours cooped up with him, the investigations I kept secret, cancelled out the benefits to me.

Now I cleaned the hamsters' cages, which they kept remarkably tidy except for the corner they used as a bathroom. I changed their bedding. I cleaned the rest of the house, too; called contractors about updating the heating system; looked into a class at the local nursery for first-time gardeners. Drew's Christmas present to me was a fancy set of gardening tools, hand-forged in Holland: a spade, a weeder, a three-tined cultivator for tilling, a narrow trowel for who-knows-what. I'd never gardened before, or wanted to.

Sometimes I stayed in the basement with the hamsters, secretly reading want ads on my laptop or in the local rag. Once I saw an opening for an assistant district attorney in Hudson, a forty-five-minute drive. Then, like a mirage, it was gone. The application was thirty-seven pages long. I filled it out anyway and signed up for email alerts about the next available position. I wondered what was happening elsewhere, in real life. After more than an hour in the basement, I'd invariably get chilled and come upstairs.

One of the best things about Henry the Eighth and Roy was that they produced Hanna's first country friend — a classmate who'd received a hamster for Christmas too. Sometimes Emily came to our house for a play date; occasionally Hanna stayed overnight at Emily's. Because our house got so chilly at night, I was reluctant to invite Emily to stay with us until we renovated the heating system in April, which I explained to Emily's mom.

One particularly frigid Saturday night when Hanna was at Emily's, Drew and I had what could only be called a romantic dinner. There was butternut squash soup, whole artichokes with herb butter, snow pea pods, a chicken recipe that was actually called 'Man-Pleasing Chicken'. The first time I made it, back in Brooklyn, the name was a joke. Now it seemed prophetic. We downed crystal glasses of Malbec. "Delicious meal," Drew said. He reached across the table and gripped my hand. "I'll do the dishes, and then perhaps we can retire early." I knew he wanted me to meet his gaze. But at that moment I realized I hadn't fed the hamsters all day. "I'll be right back," I said.

I went downstairs. The hamsters lay motionless in their cages. Without Hanna's loving touch, they had simply gone to sleep, awaiting her return, I suppose. But when I reached into their cages, I realized the reason for their stillness. They were dead. Both of them. As if they had a suicide pact. I stroked them. I talked to them. I picked up each one and listened for a heartbeat. What had I done? Drew was upstairs waiting for me. I knew he wouldn't care anyway. But Hanna would. What could I possibly tell her?

The childcare books say you should allow a child to say goodbye to a beloved pet. I know I should have waited until Hanna returned the next day to bury them. But I felt an urgency to act I hadn't experienced since we'd moved to Drew's dream house.

Were Henry the Eighth and Roy beloved? Of course they were.

Drew called down from the top of the stairs. "I'm going up." Annoyance in his voice. I told him the hamsters had died. "That's a bummer," he said. "You should complain to the pet store." He paused. "Tomorrow." Meaning, now why don't you come to bed? But I couldn't.

I was sure it was my fault.

I could have buried them in one shoebox. But surely each hamster deserved his own resting place. Most of the ground in our backyard was frozen, but I found a muddy place. The sky was heavy, glassy with stars. I wore a headlamp, a relic of our only camping trip, before we were married. I dug deep until the dirt seemed somewhat drier and grainier. I filled each shoebox with clean hamster bedding, gently placed each stiff torso in the centre, closed the shoeboxes, and set them side by side. Then I shovelled and patted the dirt on top of them, and put a stone to mark each grave.

By the time I came to bed, Drew was asleep. His back faced my side of the bed, his shoulders, even in sleep, tense with anger or suspicion. That night I didn't sleep. I worried what I would tell Hanna when she returned, how sad she would feel. The next morning, Emily's mother called to ask whether, when she dropped off Hanna, she could leave Emily with us for the day. "The girls really get along," she said. "It's cute the way they're so interested in each other's hamsters, like doting grandparents."

I told her what had happened to Henry and Roy.

"Listen. When did you bury them? They may not be dead. When goldens get cold, they hibernate; to the untutored eye, it's as if they've died. They feel stiff and lifeless—but they're not. It's how they conserve body heat. It happened to Rodrigo. We thought he had died, and I called the pet store to yell at them, and the guy told me to get my hair dryer and blow some warm air on him. It took several minutes, but, boy, did he revive. I don't know when you buried them, but you might think about . . ."

I don't remember what she said after that, other than that she would keep Hanna until suppertime.

The ground above their graves was frozen.

I took my gardening spade and I pounded. Pounded harder.

I pounded so hard Drew heard me.

He looked out the window of his study. I thought he was going to raise the window and ask me what I was doing, but he didn't.

I kept pounding until the ice began to come apart, the shards glinting like blades.

PULP *Literature*

Four awards for genre-busting fiction and poetry

The Bumblebee Flash Fiction Contest

Deadline: 15 February

Prize: $300

The Magpie Award for Poetry

Deadline: 15 April
First Prize: $500

The Hummingbird Flash Fiction Prize

Deadline: 15 June
Prize: $300

The Raven Short Story Contest

Deadline: 15 October
Prize: $300

For more information visit: pulpliterature.com/contests

Short stories, poetry, and comics you can't put down.

It Can Be Done with Words

BY ERIN MACNAIR

We know you have it in you, Thomas, even though you don't know it yet. Listen to your future readers. We know what we are talking about.

You'll know it in about two years and four months, when your agent calls and says something like 'we've done it' but you can't quite hear her words over the static inside your brain.

You dared to imagine that this book, *The Last Map*, would feed your family; it was all you were hoping to achieve. (We got this bit of information from the videos and interviews many years later in your career, where we are now, whereas you are still huffing the fumes of writerly dream ether). You have no thoughts of transcending culture, no ideas about binding humanity together in one 84,900-word paper-bound package. You knew your prose was powerful, but every writer thinks that, from what we've heard. We know that right now writing feels like extracting the marrow of your incisor tooth with a hollow needle, made worse by a sunny morning in front of an incessant blinking cursor, waiting. Later you will tell us about the anguish: pain manifesting itself in physical symptoms like neck aches, Crohn's, gout.

"It's almost like he was giving birth," your wife chimed in, in one rare interview where you told her to come up and join you on stage, flashing that toothy grin, your sharp-angled jaw handsome in that forgotten-cowboy sort of way. We wanted to dislike her because we didn't want to share our deep love. In the end, we loved her. Time to write was a luxury afforded to you by your support team, i.e. her. You told us, "Halfway through the book, divorce was imminent, but she hung on."

She concurred. "Living with a writer is awkward — all those silent spaces in their minds filled with combustible gas," she will say.

"I am a great writer because she was a great wife," you said. We cringed a little, because that's a given until we realized you actually meant it. We watched as you took a sip of tea then described the origin of Janus, our heroine, our goddess of knowledge, your hands moving through the air as if sculpting. How Janus means two-faced (we gasped at that revelation, of course! Her dual nature of light and dark, loving experimental jazz but also eating dirt when no one was looking).

You can't imagine now, in your early draft, how desperate we are for your shimmering, modern fairy tale, a panacea to our damaged psyche. We are still just a hazy vision: your appreciative readers. We will get you; we're out there — a nebula of minds waiting for transformation. But we know you aren't holding out any hope, not at this point in your career. Your incomplete biography tells us you are now in the throes of despair, soldiering on, knowing the end may never present itself. It confuses us at first; how can you not recognize what you are about to achieve? But many of us aren't writers. Your words seem effortless as if the prose came out in one beautiful tsunami.

Like the part in Chapter Eight, when the octopus gives Janus mouth-to-mouth resuscitation after she's given up and thrown her body overboard into the Pacific? Where its cephalopod consciousness imparts all of its knowledge of the sea? We especially love the paragraph where the octopus wraps Janus in a cloud of inky darkness, taking her briefly to the stars and the centre of everything, which we were relieved to see was a circle. And what about the next chapter, 'Janus Coalesces', where she can't stop rearranging her apartment, moving the shiniest of her objects closest to the door in case she has to pack up quickly, a lesson from the octopus she wholeheartedly embraces? We do that too. We can't help ourselves, knowing what we know now. About being ready for any adventure that comes our way, and how often things with shininess have weight and can be used as weapons, but only as a last resort.

We read and reread about your process. Your travels to your friend's cabin in the far Yukon, a place where one could give up if they needed to, without anyone questioning the decision. How late one night, you felt a desperate need to paint the living room a dark pink, like the inside of an ear. How you mixed the paints you found in the shed, underneath the cobwebs and rusted tools, in a metal bucket once used for milking. How afterward you dubbed this writing space 'the womb'. After this, almost everyone who could have a pink living room did, in case they too could become similarly inspired. Although you never would've paired anything in that cabin with gold or gilded flourishes, with lacquered candlesticks, as we did.

You relayed how your self-imposed silence, blanketed by the deafening snow, brought clarity as well as deep fear. There was a moment, with the shotgun? How simple it would be to wish upon the world a posthumous bestseller. Or not, you'd never know — it wouldn't matter. Lucky us, you didn't. That's why we're thinking of you right now, why we're sending our thoughts back in time, just in case you get this, to ease the passage of this book just a little.

We knew we had something special when we first opened *The Last Map*. The hand-drawn picture of your grandfather's typewriter all banged up like someone had backed over it, the ribbon spooling out like splayed intestines: we thought it represented our own lives spinning out, our ink drying up. We felt an affinity for this ancient implement; we were also waiting for intimate tapping, buttons to be pushed with resounding clacks. And on the next page, Janus, rising from the ribbon, taking shape, revealing as much to us in the cut-out negative spaces as in the filled-in ones, her body just this normal woman's, but with exceptionally kinky hair.

You taught us how to change everything, on page eighty-nine, right after the sex scene when you knew we'd be paying attention. You laid out what others thought defunct: theories about superstrings and bending of time, things we never entirely understood but had read about in *Scientific American*. Critics thought you were reaching, especially with all that 'breathing life into your previous selves' stuff — how could we go back and change who we had been? But we found we could. So many of us had read the book; we realized that we were all sharing a similar thought process; we were applying the same notions to our everyday lives. The critics backed off, became converts. You had tapped into something beyond the science: the missing piece, part love, part mathematical explanation of the path a butterfly takes.

In Janus, we have found our hopes and dreams, our losses, our failed attempts to understand humanity. But then, in the end! How you gave it all, without even knowing how we needed this to make ourselves right in the world. When Janus is looking down at the Earth like an astronaut, but it's just a miniature Earth inside a snow globe filled with sparkling confetti? We knew it was meant to be a metaphor, but everything crystallized for us: how to go forward from this moment. It wasn't just a few of us, either. It's translated into forty-seven languages — that's almost unheard-of.

Right now, at this moment in time when you are pacing in the kitchen, scratching a bit of dandruff on your head, looking for a way to make 'the map' accessible to everyone, you're wondering if anyone will read these words. If anyone will understand what it is you are trying to do. We know. We hear you. We understand now that books will change the world, stories will create a movement, not unlike the true philosophers. Only more accessible, sans jargon.

It's almost a religion. Mappers meet and regularly discuss — weekly, and often on Sundays — how to bend time, even just a little, creating shadows on the periphery. Who knew it could be done with words? Our bookmarks lie like dried tongues on the bedside tables; it doesn't matter anymore where we start and where we end *The Last Map*. It's all relevant. It's all just what we needed.

We wanted to thank you, collectively, at one proposed moment in time (this one).

You'll probably hear it as trees bending in the wind, or birdsong. We hope, for a brief moment, it will give you the courage to continue, that it will inform the pivotal moment in Chapter Three, when Janus picks herself up after a blackout in the alley behind the mall complex, next to the industrial vat of restaurant oil. We love that moment — so full of redemption. You're going to write it now. You're going to write us all in, the shadows of our former selves leaving dark stains on the pavement that we, too, can walk away from, and we love you for it.

O WORLD

Edna St Vincent Millay
& Phoebe Mol

Poet and playwright **Edna St Vincent Millay** (1892–1950) was the first woman to receive the Pulitzer Prize for poetry. The text for 'O World' is the first stanza of Millay's poem 'God's World', first published in The Lyric Year (1912).

Phoebe Mol is an artist and illustrator based in the Twin Cities. 'O World' superimposes the graceful words of Edna St Vincent Millay on an illustrated rendition of handwashing instructions. This comic was created during the first COVID-19 quarantine in March 2020, when we first had to create sharp distinctions between ourselves and our environments.

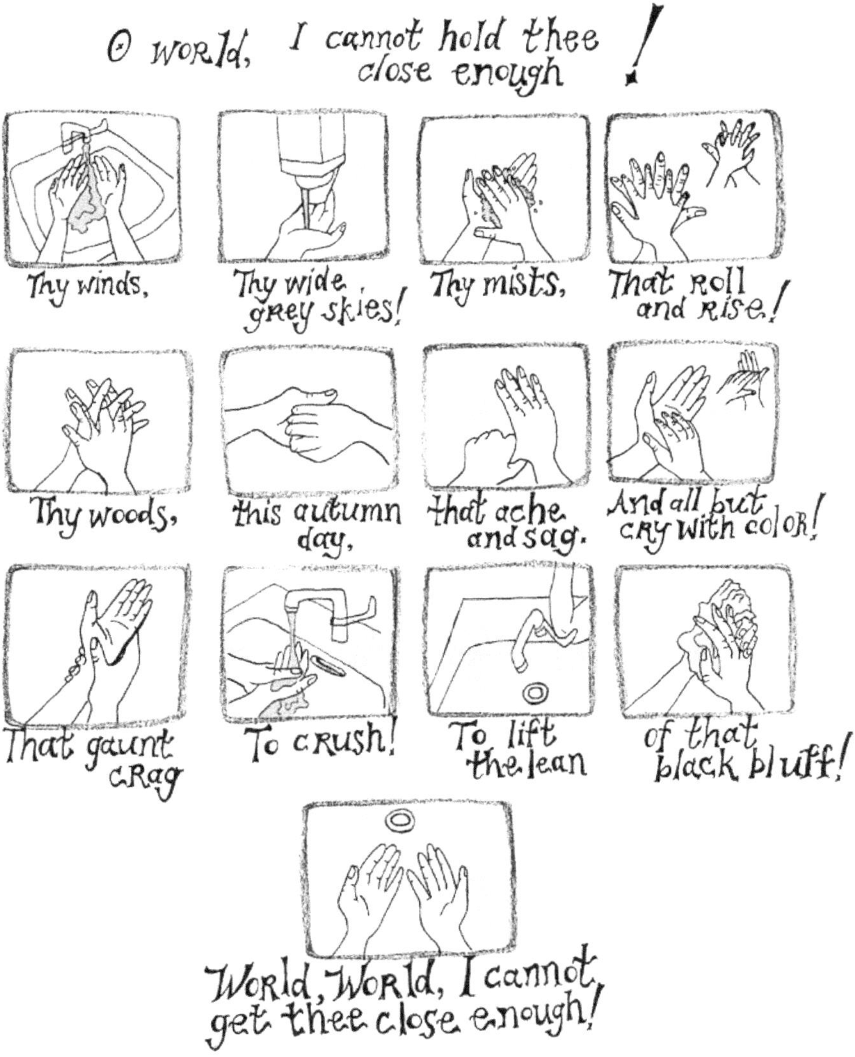

O world, I cannot hold thee close enough!

Thy winds,

Thy wide grey skies!

Thy mists,

That roll and rise!

Thy woods,

this autumn day,

that ache and sag.

And all but cry with color!

That gaunt crag

To crush!

To lift the lean

of that black bluff!

World, World, I cannot get thee close enough!

THE SHEPHERDESS: MERVEILLES

JM Landels

Former shepherdess Toinette has just arrived at the newly built palace of Versailles, along with the rest of the Countess's retinue. The small staff has barely had time to set their mistress's apartments in order when Madame falls victim to poison . . . apparently delivered via a pomander given to Marie-Claire from the debonair courtier Michel de Foix.

JM Landels is torn between travelling the world to teach writing and swordfighting, and never leaving her idyllic farm in Langley, BC. Her debut series, fantasy bestseller Allaigna's Song: Overture, and the sequel, Aria, are available from Pulp Literature Press and Amazon. You can follow her adventures with pen and sword at jmlandels.stiffbunnies.com.

ᴛHE Shepherdess: Merveilles

"Why?" I asked myself, as I frantically rubbed Madame's wrist. Why would anyone poison the Countess — if the poison was intended for her at all? And who? Claire? Her face was as grief-stricken as Mathilde's. And would she have the where-withal to insert a poisoned needle into that withered orange, even if she wanted to? Michel de Foix? The pomander had come from him — but if he knew it was poisoned, why give it to a girl he'd just met? And why carry about the lethal object anyway?

Henri returned with the surgeon — a slim man with a hooked nose and skin as dark as Henri's. He spoke with a strange fluid accent.

"Allez!" he said, shooing Mathilde away by flapping his hands. "What has happened here?"

I straightened from my crouch. "Poison," I said, and held Madame's limp palm for him to see. "I think," I added modestly.

He glanced at her hand and sniffed the air like a questing hound. He bent over, smelled her breath, if any of it there was, and tore at the neck of her chemise to expose her breast bone. He put an ear to her chest, then unfolded himself and looked me in the face. "You are not wrong, I think, but what makes you say so?"

I picked up the pomander by its ribband. He reached for it.

"Careful!" I said, and held it out of reach till it stopped spinning. I pointed to the miniscule needle tip. "Where there is one, there may be more."

He took the ribband from me with one hand and pulled an eyeglass out of his pocket with the other. "Agreed." He brought his nose an inch from the pomander. "The cloves and orange mask the scent entirely. It is a clever hiding place." He put the eyeglass away. Then he took a bowl of dusty dried rose petals from Madame's side table, emptied the contents onto the floor, and placed the pomander in the bowl.

"I will examine that later. For now, this patient clings to life with but the faintest grip."

"Will you purge her?" asked Mathilde.

"That is what your Frankish doctors would do first," he said. "Which would be worse than useless, since the poison was not ingested." He rummaged in his bag. "Phlebotomy would be their next recourse — perhaps more germane since the poison is in the blood — "

"Stop talking and just save her!" cried Claire. Her face was streaming with panicked tears. Guilt, perhaps, over having given the pomander, shock that it might have been her near death instead, along with the same fear that gripped we three women at the thought of losing our protectress.

Her comment seemed to make him move even more languidly. He pulled from his bag a small glass phial of black liquid, and a larger one of what looked like water. He poured a measure of the latter into an empty bottle, and then let a dozen drops of the black fluid fall into it. He corked the bottle, swirled it, and held the brown result to the light.

His hand went into the bag again, and this time he retrieved a cloth bundle, which he unrolled to reveal tiny knives, scissors, and other strange implements. He traced one of the large blue veins that crossed the Countess's bare chest, and then pricked it with a scalpel. A bead of blood appeared, then rolled toward the hollow between her breasts. He calmly pressed a small cloth onto it to stop the blood. "Hold this," he commanded, and I replaced his fingers with mine.

Next he retrieved what looked like a tiny water skin and poured the pale brown mixture into it. He then inserted a long piece of tapered steel into the neck and wrapped the join with waxed thread.

I could feel my heart pound through my fingers and into Madame's chest, as if it could beat for the both of us.

At last he asked me to remove my hand. The blood welled up around the small wound, and he nodded what must have been approval. He inserted the thin end of the tube into the wound, and began gently squeezing. Much of the fluid trickled down her chest, mingled with blood, but I could see the blue vein turn white as the mixture fought its way in. At last he finished, quickly pressing the cloth in place.

"Hold," he commanded once more.

He then took the phial of black liquid, pried open Madame's jaw, and let a few drops fall under her tongue. "For good measure," he said.

"Now what?" I asked.

"We wait."

The waiting was interminable. When the surgeon had cleaned and tidied his instruments, and applied a bandage to Madame's chest, he pulled the vanity's stool to her bedside, tucked his legs beneath him, tailor-style, and watched his patient. Every few minutes he reached out to feel her pulse, touch his wrist to her forehead, and write notes in a strange backward hand into a small book bound in stamped red leather. Once out of every three iterations he put a long wooden trumpet to his ear and listened to her chest.

Mathilde and Claire, unable to be still, began to put the room in order. When they made too much clatter, the surgeon shushed them.

After standing there, watching dumbly for a while, I realized no one was giving me orders and I had nothing to do. I found Henri, who had taken himself to the parlour and was pacing the carpet like a penned ewe whose lamb had slipped away. I could only be grateful he hadn't started butting the walls.

I put a hand on his elbow, stilling him. "Do you know who Michel de Foix is?"

"Bien sûr," he said with a questioning frown.

"Bring him here." I didn't say 'if you can'. The look on Henri's face said he would find the man and bring him, trussed and over one shoulder if need be. So I added, "Gently."

And then Henri was gone, and I was back to waiting, the mantelpiece clock marking the heartbeats I hoped Madame was still making.

I sat, then stood, and sat again. I went to the other chamber, spied the broom Mathilde had been using, and began sweeping the floor that had already been swept.

There was a clatter from Madame's room, and I stuck my head out in time to hear words in a foreign language that sounded like a curse. Moments later, Mathilde and Claire hurried from the room, the latter in tears. Mathilde comforted her daughter and sat her on the divan, ignoring me.

When the air was still again, I moved across the floor and entered Madame's chamber without a sound. The surgeon was listening to her heart again. I tiptoed to the armchair in the corner and sat, watching, waiting.

This time he did not take his seat, but retrieved the phial of black substance, let a few more drops fall into her mouth, frowned, and made a note in his book.

"It's not working, is it?" I asked, my voice barely louder than the murmur of the fire in the grate.

His head snapped around as if he'd just noticed me. "She is still alive," he scolded, "so yes, it is working. And no, it is not." His mobile eyebrows wrinkled toward one another. "I am beginning to suspect a second agent," he said, more to himself than to me. He paced, much as Henri had, then turned to me. "What did she eat last?"

"Nothing," I replied, "since a lunch of cold chicken and apples. But that was hours ago, and hours before she lay down."

Mathilde appeared in the doorway. "Her tonic," she said. "She takes it every evening to help her sleep. Claire says she asked for the bottle before her rest." Mathilde crossed to the vanity and opened the drawers, retrieving a brown glass bottle.

She held it up to the dimming light from the window, showing that less than a quarter remained. "This was full this morning."

The surgeon snatched the bottle from her hand and uncorked it, sniffing. He poured a drop onto his palm, touched his tongue to it, and sprang to action. He removed a new phial from his bag. When he uncorked it, the stench made my gorge rise. He waved it under Madame's nose and, when that had no effect, poured a dose into her mouth.

"Quick, help me sit her up," he said to me.

I raced to Madame's other side and pulled her limp arm over my shoulder, bracing her into a sitting position while the surgeon held her head and massaged her throat.

"Wait," he said to me, and I waited. "You," he said to Mathilde, "get a chamber pot."

This waiting seemed as long as the prior half hour, though I'm certain it was only a minute or so before Madame's shoulders shuddered and heaved.

"Now. Roll her onto her side."

It nearly broke my back, so awkward was my position, but I managed to ease her down and over. By now I was kneeling on the bed, my skirts caught under me and tugging at my waist, stretching to hold her shoulder while the surgeon held her head. As her body convulsed, I was dragged forward and down, suddenly aware once more of the letter opener sliding under my stomacher. Another convulsion, and she vomited into the pot Mathilde held, just as Michel de Foix entered the room.

I was the only person who saw Michel. The others were watching with faces either horrified or satisfied by the violent convulsions crashing through Madame's body. But I was at her back and glanced up as Henri escorted the smaller man through the door.

Henri's shoulders dropped as relief washed through him. Michel wrenched his arm away from Henri's grip and rushed to the foot of the bed, then took a step back as Madame vomited again. Michel's face went through several cycles of shock, concern, and revulsion in this brief moment, but I could not tell if guilt was mixed in there.

I glanced back down at Madame, whose shoulders were heaving as she gasped for breath. The surgeon reached out fastidiously to wipe her mouth with a square of linen, and then he put two fingers behind her jaw to feel her heartbeat.

He nodded at Mathilde, who removed the chamber pot, and then at me. I moved backward, still kneeling on the bed, and allowed the Countess to roll onto her back.

Her eyes were open, though only just. The physician glanced up at the crowd around Madame's bedside. "What is this, a salon? Out!" He waved the soiled handkerchief. "You" — he looked at Claire — "bring warm water, and you" — this time his gaze fell on Mathilde — "tea with plenty of honey, if such a thing can be found. The rest of you, go!"

I shuffled backward off the bed and straightened my rumpled skirts, wishing I were wearing my plain wool rather than this borrowed finery, and made to follow Michel and Henri toward the parlour.

Henri paused in the doorway, blocking it with his bulk. "Monsieur le chirugien," he said, "will she die?"

"We will all die, sir," said the surgeon, not looking up from his examination of Madame's pale face.

I gave Henri a shove and pushed past him and Michel, dragging them into the parlour.

Michel's face was ghostly pale, his blue eyes wide and naïve.

"Did you tell him?" I asked Henri.

"Tell me what?" Michel looked years younger than the worldly courtier we'd met on the stairs today.

"That it was the pomander you gave Marie-Claire which poisoned Catrin," growled Henri, looking and sounding much like a bristling mastiff.

"Pomander?" His gaze flicked from Henri to me. "The orange? But how?"

"We thought perhaps you could tell us that, m'sieur," I replied. "I am from the country and have seldom seen oranges, but I did not know they grew poison needles."

He turned and made his way to the settee, grasping its carved cherrywood back like an old man as he lowered himself into it. By the time he faced us again, his countenance was the colour of tallow.

"Athenaïs," he whispered, and rubbed a hand over his face. "I … took it from her this morning."

"Athenaïs," growled Henri. "The Marquise de Montespan? What do you mean, 'took it from her'?"

"Ah …" Michel shook his head. "That I cannot tell you, m'sieur."

The surgeon emerged from Madame's bedroom, holding his bag and the small porcelain dish containing the pomander. "She is resting," he said, "but someone should stay at her side tonight."

Claire moved before I could answer. "I will," she said, and shut the door behind her.

The surgeon put the dish down on the ebony side table and drew a footstool near to sit upon. The orange shone gold in the light of the two lamps on the mantel.

"Bring me one of those." I brought a heavy-bottomed lamp down, turning the wick to give more light. There wasn't room for both the lamp and the dish on the small side table, so I rested half the base on the table and continued supporting it with my hand.

With a knife and a pair of tweezers, the surgeon teased the orange, rolling it on its knobbled surface till the clove that held the needle was on top. He wrested the clove from the orange skin with the tweezers, pulling it straight out and leaving an inch-long needle still protruding from the orange. I glanced at Mathilde and the other two men, all of whom held horror on their faces, but none more than Michel de Foix.

The surgeon placed the clove into the dish and grasped the needle with his tweezers, pulling that free as well. From the hole in the orange, a thick red substance oozed.

"What … is that?" Michel's blue eyes were wide.

The surgeon held the needle to the light, then to his nose. "I have two strong guesses and a third possibility. I will have to take it to my laboratory to be certain." He placed the needle in the dish beside the clove and laid his instruments down as well. "It is a poison that should have killed her if not for the opium that had already dulled her nerves. Or," he said, frowning, "it is a harmless hallucinogen that combined with her tonic to nearly kill her. I will have to discover which."

He stood, picked up his bag in one hand and the dish in the other, and left without a word of farewell.

"Which is it?" I asked Michel as I returned the lamp to its place above the fire.

He removed his wig—a shockingly familiar gesture that I had neither the breeding nor the energy to find shocking—and ran a hand through the short blond hair underneath.

"That is an answer I would very much like to have myself, mademoiselle."

"You knew nothing of this?" said Henri, his voice heavy with scepticism.

"Would I carry a lethal thing like that hanging from my pocket if I did?"

"I don't know," growled Henri, rising to loom over the other man. "How often do you poison others?"

"Enough, Henri," I said. "He gave it to Claire on the stairs. How could he know she'd give it to Madame?"

"The surgeon said it may have been a harmless potion. Such as the women in Saint Antoine sell to maidens to turn their loves' regard. Perhaps it's how he seduces his prey here at court."

"Ça suffit!" I exclaimed. "Madame is late for her appointment with Monsieur Colbert. Perhaps you should go and beg his forgiveness?"

"You go," said Henri. "I'll not let this one from my sight."

I walked to Henri, looked up into his face towering above mine, and spun him around by his elbow. "I wouldn't have a clue how to find him in this palace. Monsieur de Foix will not leave my sight." I gave Henri's massive back a shove and sent him reluctantly to the door.

"Now." I spread my skirts and sat on the divan, patting the seat beside me as I did when wringing the truth of some misdeed from one of my younger siblings. "You had best tell me what you would not tell him. Where did the pomander, and the poison, come from?"

Michel bowed, having recovered some of his poise with the departure of Henri, spread his coattails, and sat at the other end of the divan.

"In faith, mademoiselle. I took it from a bowl full of the same in the chamber of Madame de Montespan this very morning."

"With or without her knowledge?"

He hesitated. "That would be telling too much."

"Do you think she knows of the needle?"

He shook his head. "I cannot say."

"Cannot, or will not?"

"In truth, I cannot."

"A bowl of them, you say …" I let the question dangle.

He put his hands on his face. "They could all be so tainted—or none but that one. And whether she knows or not is the difference between complicity and victimhood."

"We had best find out, then."

"We?"

"I promised Henri you would not leave my sight."

De Foix swept the floor with the plume of his hat as he bowed to the lady's maid who opened the door to the Marquise de Montespan's apartments. The motion drew the eye down to his calves, clad in silk hose. I noticed that he turned his front foot sideways, further accentuating the calf and the red heels of his silver-buckled shoes.

"Daphné," he declared, taking the maid's hand as he straightened and bringing it to his lips. "You are as graceful a sight as your namesake."

A flush of pink travelled up her neck. "Madame has already gone for dinner, Chevalier."

"What, and left you here?"

Her eyes fell. "I have work to do, sir."

"Well, mademoiselle, would you mind terribly much if my … sister … and I rested here for a moment? These shoes"—he held out a foot and twisted his ankle to and fro—"are new, and the walk from the north wing is hellish."

"Of course, sir." She held open the door and let us into the apartment, which was larger and far more grandly furnished than Madame's. "You must excuse me, though. I am still tidying from her toilette." She hurried into the adjoining room.

"Sister?" I murmured when she was out of hearing.

"Anything else and she'd be jealous."

"So it was Daphné, not the Marquise, you were visiting when you took the orange this morning?"

His eyes slid to the door through which she had disappeared. "Oui et non. I believe her absence at dinner tonight is a punishment."

"For dallying with you?"

"For not dallying with His Majesty last night."

I was thoroughly confused. "But the Marquise is his mai-tresse-en-titre, is she not?"

"Her star is falling, and that of the Marquise de Maintenon is rising. But His Majesty's eye has always wandered. Athenaïs would prefer it wandered to a servant of her choice rather than to the governess of her children."

"And what is your role in all this?"

He sighed. "I seem to have written a poem that came into the wrong hands." He looked sheepish. "I had brought it to Athenaïs to read, but I gave it to Daphné to deliver."

"And Daphné thought it was for her?" As unfamiliar as I was with the court, even I knew an alliance between an ambitious chevalier and a lady's maid was unlikely.

He shrugged. "I confess I may have flattered her one too many times."

I narrowed my eyes. "Weren't you just today petitioning for a marriage?"

"Indeed," his head fell, the curls of his wig swinging. "And lost. Angelique is to wed an English duke."

"My condolences," I said without feeling.

"Thank you. It is my own tragic fault, though," he said, touching the corner of his eye with the lace points of his voluminous cuff. "Had I not lingered here this morning, Angelique's hand—and fortune—would have been mine.

"But enough self-pity," he continued. "We need to see those oranges. There is a chaise percée in the closet of the Marquise's room. Ask to use it, and I will distract Daphné."

I scratched on the door. "Mademoiselle?" I called.

"Oui, Mada—moiselle?" answered Daphné, her head emerging from the doorway in a cloud of perfume and hastily applied powder.

"My brother tells me there is a chair ..." I had no idea of the protocol around asking to use another person's commode.

"*Bien sûr.*" She ushered me in, and showed me the door to the closet.

"Thank you, ma chère," I replied with what I hoped was appropriate condescension for the sister of a chevalier speaking to a maid.

"De rien, Mademoiselle de Foix," she replied, and left me alone.

It would be suspicious not to leave something in the pot, so I hoisted my skirts and sat upon the cold, pink-flowered seat of the chaise. I poured some washing water in for good measure afterwards.

I tiptoed out of the closet into the bedchamber, which was now deserted. The bowl of oranges was nowhere to be seen. As I emerged from the chamber of the Marquise, I caught Michel's eye over the shoulder of Daphné, who was seated upon his lap.

"Daphné, my sweet," he said, taking one of her side curls and pulling it through his fingers. "The orange you gave me this morning—there was a bowl full of them." He released the lock of hair, which bounced into place like a spring. "Where is it?"

She put a hand to the side of her head, rearranging the artful cascade of her Fontange hairdo. "So greedy, Chevalier," she said, tapping him on the nose. "Is one not enough?"

"Answer the question, minx, or I shall undo your toilette and search for them myself." He plucked the ribbon of her chemise. She gave a small squeal, and I cleared my throat to remind them both I stood in the room. She jumped to her feet, readjusting her ribbons.

"Since you must know," she replied with a pout, "they were a gift from the Madame de Maintenon. Madame returned them this afternoon. She would be most annoyed if she knew you'd taken one."

No doubt she would, I thought. I locked eyes with Michel, wondering if he was going to take this maid into confidence. Instead he languidly stood and kissed Daphné's fingertips with a bow. "We've taken too much of your time already, chère mademoiselle. Come, sister, we will be late for dinner." He offered me his arm. I took it in what I hoped was a gentlewoman's fashion and let him lead me from the room.

"Smaller steps," he whispered to me once in the hall. "You must appear to glide, as if your feet do not touch the ground beneath your skirts.

"Now that you are my sister, we will have to work quickly. You must be presented to the Queen, and, alas, your mistress is in no state to do that."

"But the oranges —?" I wondered how he could have forgotten the purpose of our visit so quickly.

"Have gone to their owner. If Françoise" —he must have meant Madame de Maintenon— "sent poisoned pomanders to Athenaïs and Athenaïs sent them back, no one is in danger. If Athenaïs poisoned them before sending them back," he said, shrugging, "there is little we can do. I'm not so close to Maintenon—I can't burst into her apartments with accusations of poison, especially when only one of the fruits may have been so. No, we can only hope such was the case. And if one of Françoise's household falls ill, we can be glad there is a surgeon already familiar with the substance near at hand."

We turned a corner and encountered a pair of courtiers in extreme finery, strolling down the hall. Michel stopped, bowed low, and tugged on my wrist. I curtsied.

"De Foix," said the silver-wigged one with a crescent-shaped patch on his cheek.

"Monsieur," said Michel, "allow me to present my sister, Mademoiselle de Foix."

"I didn't know you had one, de Foix, said the chestnut-wigged man beside him. He was shorter even than Michel, despite heels that were at least a handsbreadth tall. He took my hand, kissing it as a wave of perfume washed from his wig. "The Chevalier de Lorraine is at your service, ma belle."

Michel reached out and took my hand back, tucking it under his arm. "She is freshly emerged from the convent."

The silver-wigged one pursed his rouged lips and turned to the Chevalier de Lorraine. "What de Foix is saying, my dear, is that she is a rose unplucked, and he'll thank you to leave her thus." The smile he turned upon me was somewhere between lascivious and disapproving. "Have you met my wife yet?"

I curtsied again. "No, m'sieur."

"See to it she does. Au'voir, Chevalier. Mademoiselle."

The pair of gentlemen moved on.

"Ventre!" said Michel, when we were out of earshot.

"What?"

"I had hoped to introduce you first to the Queen, but now we haven't much time. The Duke and his wife don't talk much, but either he or Lorraine will mention you sooner or later, and you'll need to see Madame."

"Madame?" I was confused.

"Not Catherine," he said. "Madame, the king's sister-in-law."

"So that was … ?"

"Oui, the Duc d'Orleans. The King's brother, Monsieur."

He picked up his pace as we continued, forcing me to trot to keep up. So much for gliding, I thought.

The following morning, my mistress was much recovered— enough to sit up in her bed and sip a small cup of hot black liquid I later learned was Turkish coffee. In fact, she looked remarkably well for someone who was on Death's lintel the day before.

As I cleared away the tiny porcelain cup and saucer, wondering where I'd encountered that intense aroma before, there was a scratch at the door.

It was the surgeon, come to check on his patient. After measuring her pulse and listening to her chest with his trumpet, his assessment mirrored my own. "Remarkable."

"Indeed, m'sieur," replied Madame with a smile. "I am indebted to your unparalleled skills."

He waved a hand. "It is true that none other at court knows my techniques, but I refer to your recovery, Countess."

"Madame has the constitution of an ox," said Mathilde as she bustled in with an armload of pillows. "Your pardon, Madame."

"Dear Mathilde," said the Countess, leaning forward so Mathilde could replace and rearrange the pillows behind her.

"There is precious little you could say to offend me. "Monsieur." She addressed the surgeon as she settled back. "I assume you have come for your payment. Mathilde can address that for you. Mathilde, be sure to add a few écus to whatever he asks."

"Madame is generous, but I have come with more than an open palm. It is about the poison."

He removed a box from his bag and opened it to reveal the remains of the orange, neatly sectioned. In the centre of the blossom-like array lay a collection of tiny brass wheels and springs.

"What is it?" she asked.

"A delivery mechanism. Timed, I believe."

"Who could create clockwork so small?" she asked.

"That, I could not tell you. But if you find the one who made this device, you will be one step closer to knowing who set this trap."

"This age of miracles and marvels," she sighed, and let her head sink back on the pillow. "And what of the poison itself?"

"It is one that should have killed you within seconds, Madame. That it did not—"

"Is due to the excessive amount of my tonic I consumed yesterday? Or my constitution of an ox?"

"On that, I can only speculate." He bowed again. "If I might have a sample of your cordial, I could study it further."

She opened her eyes halfway and smiled as her head gave the barest shake. "That is an old family recipe. One that I am not at liberty to share. Thank you, monsieur. I am in your debt. Leave the box."

Her eyes closed again, and I took the box away to her dressing table before escorting the surgeon to the drawing room, where Mathilde provided him with a purse and marked the transaction in Madame's ledger.

As he prepared to leave, I could keep my curiosity quiet no longer. "The poison, sir — it smelled of apple blossoms, and something else?"

He turned his dark brown eyes on me. "And how would you know that?"

"I … I could smell it when I picked up the pomander. And again when you opened the box."

"That is a sensitive nose you have, to smell it through the orange and cloves. It was a compounded substance: arsenic, which is what gave you your hint of apples, and scorpion venom."

"Scorpion?"

"It is a creature that lives in the desert where I come from. It looks like a langoustine, but much smaller … and deadlier. They are not native here, and the venom degrades quickly. Whoever compounded it must keep live scorpions."

"Why did you not tell Madame that?"

"I believe the Countess has all the information she needs about what poisons abound at court and who concocts them." He leaned closer. "Consider this, mademoiselle: the only reason she survived was because her cordial contains the antidote."

He bowed deeply. "You have a curious mind and talented senses, mademoiselle. If you tire of being a lady's maid, consider apprenticing as a pharmaciste."

With that, he left, leaving me no less curious than before.

§

The Shepherdess *will continue in* Pulp Literature *Issue 32, Autumn 2021.*

THE ARTISTS

Weiwei Xu

Cover artist, Superbloom

Weiwei is a self-taught Chinese-Canadian artist who loves to play with Chinese folklore and casual fantasy in their work. Weiwei has some sort of science degree, which, while not particularly useful, occasionally manifests in their art. When they are not drawing, they can be found making noodles or deep diving into local forest trails and internet rabbit holes. You can find more of their work at @peevishpants on Twitter, @itscoolguylink on Instagram, or theweiweixu.portfoliobox.net/home.

Superbloom is an ode to wanderlust in solitude and the joy of discovering new places. Real-life superblooms happen when a lot of native desert flowers suddenly sprout simultaneously, usually after heavy rains. They're beautiful to behold, but a tourist influx will destroy them — it's much better to enjoy superblooms through art and photos than to trample them in person!

Phoebe Mol

Artist, 'O World'

Phoebe Mol is an artist and illustrator based in the Twin Cities. She tells stories primarily with pen and ink, watercolour, and coloured pencil. Her work explores memory, life and decay, and the interplay between environment and experience. She recently provided art direction and illustration for the community food justice group Beaverton Food Project and has worked to create recipe art for Common Harvest Farm and educational illustrations for the German textbook Grenzenlos Deutsch. She is also an arts educator at a progressive arts studio for artists with disabilities. Find more of her work at phoebemol.com.

Mel Anastasiou
In-house illustrator

Mel Anastasiou loves drawing for *Pulp Literature* because she loves the stories she illustrates. She draws in black and white, working from imagination and inspired by details from Renaissance compositions. You can find illustrations, writing tips, and news about her books and novellas at melanastasiou.wordpress.com, and see more of her artwork on Facebook at Bird and Branch Artwork.

HALL OF FAME

These are the heroes — the Patrons and Pulp Literati whose monthly support helped bring you this issue. Please lift your glasses and give them a rousing cheer!

The Shareholders
Rapscallion

The Brewers
Robin McGillveray
A Bursewicz

The Landlords
Isabel Cushey
Dana Tye Rally

The Innkeepers
Ada Maria Soto
Margot Landels
Ev Bishop
Shannon Saunders
Roger & Anne Anastasiou
Kevin Harris
Gillian Gardiner
Megan Shaw
Susan Jackson
Megan Dahl

The Cicerones
Elsa Carruthers

The Bartenders
Alana Krider

Richard Gropp
Ron Graves
Kristen Mah
Robert Bose
Victoria McAuley
Dave Wayne
Scott F Gray
Michelle Balfour
Abigail Bruce
Vernice Dietra Malik
Katriona Greenmoor
AD Bane
KT Wagner
Michael Weckworth
Deepthi Atukorala
Margot Spronk
Margaret Elliott
Peter Halasz
Bjarne Hansen
Leny Wagner
Kain Stewart
Chris Olee
kc dyer
Kimberley Aslett
Jan Fagan
Ken Oakes
Brighton Hugg
Jeffrey Parent

The Regulars
CC Humphreys
Marta Salek
Rina Piccolo
Emily Lonie
Jenny Blackford
Jain Cairns
Akemi Art
BC
Miriam Zibkoff
Meredith Frazier
Catherine Levinson
Vera
Charity Tahmaseb
Alexander Langer
Marilyn Holt
Risa Wolf
Barbara Pengelly
David Perlmutter
Christine McCullough
Ishbel Newstead

The Clientele
Ray Hsu
Melissa Hudson

If you would like to join the ranks of these worthies, you can become a patron on Patreon at patreon.com/pulplit or join the Pulp Literati through our website at pulpliterature.com/join-pulp-literati/.

HELP WANTED?

If you are a new writer, or a writer with a troublesome manuscript, EVENT's **Reading Service for Writers** may be just what you need.

Manuscripts will be edited by one of EVENT's editors and receive an assessment of 700-1000 words, focusing on such aspects of craft as voice, structure, rhythm and point of view.

eventmagazine.ca

MARKETPLACE

*B*OOKS

Advent *by Michael Kamakana* • We thought we knew what the aliens wanted. Think again. • pulpliterature.com/advent

Allaigna's Song: Aria *by JM Landels* • The long-awaited sequel to the bestselling *Allaigna's Song: Overture*. •pulpliterature.com/allaignas-song

The Extra: A Monument Studios Mystery *by Mel Anastasiou* • Extra Frankie Ray gets her big break on the Silver Screen, until Murder steals the scene. pulpliterature.com/the-extra

The Labours of Mrs Stella Ryman: Further Fairmount Mysteries *by Mel Anastasiou* • Trapped in a down-at-the-heels care home. You'd be cranky too. • pulpliterature.com/stella-ryman-and-the-fairmount-manor-mysteries

What the Wind Brings *by Matthew Hughes* • Winner of the 2020 Endeavour Award • pulpliterature.com/product-category/novels/matthew-hughes

The Writer's Boon Companion *by Mel Anastasiou* • Thirty Days Towards an Extraordinary Volume • pulpliterature.com/subscribe/the-bookstore

*B*OOKSTORES

Book Warehouse • 632 Broadway W, Vancouver, BC V5Z 1G1 • 604-872-5711 bookwarehouse.ca

Myth Hawker Travelling Bookstore • Canadian authors• Canadian content• small and independent press • mythhawker.ca

Phoenix On Bowen • 992 Dorman Rd, Bowen Island, BC V0N 1G0 • 604-947-2793

Village Books & Coffee House • 130-12031 First Ave, Richmond, BC V7E 3M1 • 604-272-6601 • villagebooks@shaw.ca

Western Sky Books • 2132-2850 Shaughnessy St, Port Coquitlam, BC V3C 6K5 • 604-461-5602 • store.westernskybooks.com

White Dwarf / Dead Write Books • 3715 10th Ave W, Vancouver, BC V6R 2G5 • 604-228-8223 • whitedwarf@deadwrite.com

*C*ONFERENCES AND EVENTS

Word on the Lake • May 2021 • Salmon Arm, BC • wordonthelakewritersfestival.com

Creative Ink Festival • May 2021 Burnaby, BC • creativeinkfestival.com

When Words Collide • August 2021 Calgary, AB • whenwordscollide.org

Wine Country Writers' Festival 24–25 September 2021 • Penticton, BC winecountrywritersfestival.ca

Surrey International Writers' Conference 22–24 October 2021 • Virtual Event • siwc.ca

Do you have a **story to tell?**
We can help!

Dreamers is dedicated to heartfelt writing. Visit our site for:

- Therapeutic Writing
- Poems & Stories
- Content Marketing
- Creative Nonfiction
- Writing Workshops
- Contests & Anthologies
- Residencies & Retreats
- ...and so much more!

www.DreamersWriting.com

GEIST
go to geist.com/subscribe
or call 1-888-GEIST-EH
Keep it weird.
Subscribe today!
FACT + FICTION • NORTH of AMERICA

onspec
the canadian magazine of the fantastic
Expect the unexpected.
www.onspec.ca

MICHAEL
KAMAKANA
ADVENT
WE THOUGHT WE KNEW WHAT THEY WANTED
WE WERE WRONG

The Digest
Enthusiast
Book Thirteen
Jan. 2021
Steve Carper
Peter Enfantino
Emily Hockaday
Gary Lovisi
Vince Nowell, Sr.
Jack Seabrook
Robert Snashall
Joe Wehrle, Jr.

MYTH HAWKER
· TRAVELLING BOOKSTORE ·

"Myth Hawker has a crush on the
underdog: the small press, the
overlooked author, the independent
bookstore, and the vast, undiscovered
treasures of small-scale publishing."

Myth Hawker travels the length & breadth
of Canada, popping up at conventions &
festivals in every province, showcasing the
work of small press & independent
Canadian authors. Follow them online to
see where they're popping up next!

www.mythhawker.com   a Mythhawker

JUNE 2020
MYSTERY WEEKLY
Magazine

Marshal Han was
wrong. Sometimes
evidence did fly
away...

Featuring
Tammy Huffman
Robert Lopresti
Arthur Vidro
Allan Durand
Luke Foster
Carl Robinette
Martin Hill Ortiz

THE CALCULUS OF
KARMA
by M. C. Tuggle

WRITE
LIKE NO ONE IS
WATCHING
PACIFIC NORTHWEST WRITERS VIRTUAL CONFERENCE
SEPT. 15TH -19TH
Register, pricing and info at
PNWA.ORG/CONFERENCEPL
PNWA
a writer's resource

Allaigna's Song
Aria
JM Landels

Allaigna's Song
Overture
AMAZON
#1
BESTSELLER
JM Landels

CONTESTS

Pulp Literature runs four annual contests for poetry, flash fiction, and short stories. For contest guidelines, prizes, and entry fees, see pulpliterature.com/contests.

THE MAGPIE AWARD FOR POETRY
Contest opens: 1 March 2021
Deadline: 15 April 2021
Winner notified: 15 May 2021
Winner published: Issue 32, Autumn 2021
Prize: $500

THE HUMMINGBIRD FLASH FICTION PRIZE
Contest opens: 1 May 2021
Deadline: 15 June 2021
Winner notified: 15 July 2021
Winner published: Issue 33, Winter 2022
Prize: $300

THE RAVEN SHORT STORY CONTEST
Contest opens: 1 September 2021
Deadline: 15 October 2021
Winner notified: 15 November 2021
Winner published: Issue 34, Spring 2022
Prize: $300

ℬᴇᴄᴏᴍᴇ ᴀ Pᴀᴛʀᴏɴ ᴏꜰ Pᴜʟᴘ Lɪᴛᴇʀᴀᴛᴜʀᴇ

By supporting *Pulp Literature* on Patreon with $2 or more per month, you will be laying the foundation for a secure future for the magazine, as well as ensuring that you never miss an issue! Your subscription includes four big issues of short stories, novellas, poetry, comics, and novel excerpts, delivered to your door or electronic mailbox each year. **Find us at patreon.com/pulplit**

If you prefer to subscribe through our website, go to pulpliterature. com/subscribe.

Or you can send a cheque with the form below to
Subscriptions, Pulp Literature Press, 21955 16 Ave, Langley BC, V2Z 1K5, Canada

---

Don't miss an issue!

- ❑ **Send me 2 years (8 issues) at the special rate of $90** (save $30)*
- ❑ **Send me 1 year (4 issues) for $50** (save $10)*
- ❑ **Send me 2 years of digital issues for $30** (save $9.92)
- ❑ **Send me 1 year of digital issues for $17.50** (save $2.47)

Name: ____

Address: ____

City: _________________________________ Prov. / State: _________

Postal code: ______________ Country:___________________

Email: ____

- ❑ Payment enclosed
- ❑ Bill me
- ❑ New
- ❑ Renewal

Make cheques payable in Canadian funds to J. Landels. Include email address for digital editions and Paypal billing, or subscribe at www.pulpliterature.com.

*for postage outside Canada add $20 per year in North America or $36 per year overseas.